ORCAS
INTRUDER

Books by Laura Gayle

The Chameleon Chronicles:
Orcas Intrigue
Orcas Intruder
Orcas Investigation
Orcas Illusion (forthcoming)

ORCAS
INTRUDER

Book 2 of
The Chameleon Chronicles

Laura Gayle

Book View Café Publishing Cooperative

Orcas Intruder, by Laura Gayle

Copyright © 2018 by Shannon Page and Karen G. Berry
Edited by Chaz Brenchley

Cover art and design by Mark J. Ferrari
Interior design by Shannon Page

Second Edition

ISBN: 978-1-61138-726-1

www.bookviewcafe.com
Book View Café Publishing Cooperative

Wednesday

CHAPTER 1

This wasn't what I had in mind.

I'd envisioned a cozy family Thanksgiving on Orcas Island. Something warm and golden, a little fuzzy around the edges. In my vision, my parents and I sat happily around the guesthouse dinner table, all of us wearing hand-knit sweaters, maybe. We'd be drinking spiced cider and laughing over a game of Scrabble while the delicious aroma of roasting turkey drifted in from the kitchen to tantalize us. After I pulled out a knuckle-biting victory, we'd gather around the laptop and Skype with my world-traveling brother.

"My mother was supposed to be here, but they missed the three-forty ferry," I said to JoJo, who had arranged his splendid collection of limbs in the corner of the guesthouse kitchen in order to watch me cook. Or prepare to cook, actually—apparently I was supposed to brine this thing? How do you brine something that's bigger than every pot you own? "I really have no idea what I'm doing."

"Really." His eyes danced, his expression amused and his tone sardonic. "I'd never have guessed."

"I must be a natural." I peered at the little plastic-y directions that had come with the turkey, dangerously close to calling the 800 number to beg someone on the other end of the line to helicopter in and do this for me.

"You're dripping."

"Ugh. So I am." The directions were covered with turkey water or juice or whatever you called the disgusting liquid surrounding a raw turkey. So much botulism or ptomaine or trichinosis in that juice, and James was watching me, whiskers twitching, waiting to dart in and get at the drips. "Don't even think about it, James."

He swished his tail and kept watching.

"I have an idea," drawled JoJo, blinking those luminous eyes. I was positive this man had ideas, he absolutely *reeked* of ideas, and the worst part was that he seemed to give *me* ideas. And I was not ready for *any ideas at all*, thank you very much.

JoJo had been tailing me around since he'd arrived the day before. Every time I looked up, there he was, looking rumpled and rich and irresistible. Tinkering with his flawless car when I went to get the mail. Drinking coffee on the back deck when I came over to triple-check that all was well for his parents' arrival.

Even now, as he leaned against the wall by my kitchen window, he looked like he was posing for maximum advantage; his hair lifted by a breeze from the back door, his body positioned in such a way as to show off his broad shoulders, the sun dancing on highlights that were awfully perfect, if they were indeed natural.

It was enough to make me drop the roasting directions. James leapt upon them and carried them right out the back door.

I let out a stream of invective, and then I blushed. "I'm sorry. I was clueless before. Now I'm desperate. And Mom won't be here till like dinnertime!"

"Cam, Cam, Cam." JoJo gave his head of gold-kissed curls a little shake and started scrolling on his phone. "We have the Internet. Or rather, what passes for Internet on this barren rock of an island. Do you remember how much the turkey weighs?"

"Nineteen pounds."

That stopped him. "Nineteen pounds? Why on Earth…"

I gaped back at him. "What? Is that a lot?"

"A lot?" He burst out laughing. "No, not if you're planning on hosting the whole island."

Well, now Mom's chuckle on the phone the other day made more sense. "Um, leftovers are good?" If I was blushing before, I was aflame now. "Yeah. Leftover turkey. Sandwiches. You know?"

"Calm down, calm down. I was curious, that's all. You don't strike me as much of a carnivore, to be honest. You have a sort of…"—he appraised me from below his bountiful, tawny lashes—"vegetarian air about you."

I stared at the pink mountain of turkey meat on the counter, shuddering at its bumpy skin and strange yellow patches. Hard to believe this was going to be delicious turkey sandwiches in a few days. "I am *not* a vegetarian. But if I said I was, would you cook this for me?"

We were both laughing when a shadow filled the doorframe. Lisa Cannon, looking so little like Lisa Cannon that I almost didn't recognize her. She was trembling, pale, her hair all crazy rather than artfully tousled. Her eyes, blind with terror, darted to mine. "Cam? Oh Cam, I'm…my home, there's…there's been an intruder and…"

JoJo's voice was deep with alarm. "An intruder, Lisa? At your house?"

Lisa stepped in and saw JoJo, then. Her expression of terror melted into actual tears. She ran to his arms. "JoJo! I'm so glad you're here!"

He pulled her close; she trembled in his grasp, I could see it from across the room. Lisa Cannon trembled! I just stared at them both for a long moment, until he relaxed his grip and she drew back.

"I'll go check it out," he said, manfully.

"Oh, no," she said, blinking away tears and seeming to come into better possession of herself. She even reached up and ran a hand through her wild mess of hair. "It's not safe."

"Did you call Ki—I mean, the cops?" I asked, my hand automatically going under my sweatshirt to my still-bandaged upper arm. The wound smarted a little less every day. I dreaded getting the stitches out, though that wouldn't be till next week.

Lisa turned to me, wide-eyed. "No. I just ran over here, as soon as I saw…"

"What did you see?" JoJo asked. "Is someone still there?"

"I don't think so. I don't know." She was calming more each moment, and standing very close to JoJo. Their hands nearly brushed. It looked very…intimate. "But I didn't stay around to find out. They could be."

"We should call 911, then," he said, somehow becoming even taller. He reached into his pocket and pulled out his cell phone.

"No," Lisa and I both said, together.

JoJo gaped at both of us. "Why not?"

I shook my head and looked helplessly at Lisa. She shrugged at me, equally at a loss. Finally, I managed, "There's…been kind of a lot going on around here." My hand went to my upper arm again. At least my skin wasn't prickling; I was *so* not ready to chameleon in front of JoJo Brixton.

He turned to Lisa. "A lot of what, Lisa?" His voice was low, familiar. "It isn't—"

"No—yes—I don't know—Sheila—she caused some trouble," Lisa stammered. "She's gone now."

"Gone?"

"They think she's dead," I managed. "She kidnapped me, and…other stuff. I got shot."

"*Shot?*" JoJo still held his phone, looking ready to punch the buttons at any moment. "You've been shot and you didn't *say* anything?"

"I'm still getting my own mind around it. I thought your parents would…"

"We've been hoping things would get a little quieter around here," Lisa said, taking a deep breath. She smoothed her hair again. "We've had rather too many authorities coming and going. I'm sure I just got spooked. It can't be Sheila, back from the dead. It was probably just…one of the actors, looking for something." She gave us a brave smile. "I'm sorry to give you both a fright."

"Well, I'm going to check it out," JoJo said, shoving his phone back into his pocket.

"I'm going with you," I blurted out. *Why?* I immediately asked myself. Was I a moron? Did I *want* more intrigue in my life? Yet I followed him to the back door.

Lisa grabbed my hand. "I'm coming too."

"Safety in numbers," I said.

We followed him across the lawn, to the path through the trees. Of course JoJo would know about the path between their estates…he and Lisa clearly knew each other well. I glanced around, but saw no sign of my little fuzzy orange directions-thief.

When we emerged at Lisa's, I saw that her front door was wide open. She was still holding my hand; now she squeezed it and let go. "Did you leave it that way?" I asked her, as JoJo strode toward the open door.

"I did," she confessed, looking sheepish. "I got home and saw, and just panicked and ran to your place."

JoJo took a step inside, and halted. We stopped behind him on the porch. "My goodness," he said, turning back to us. "That's… quite a mess."

I looked over his shoulder. The house was a shambles. Her exquisite front table was on its side in the entryway, a hand-thrown vessel of expensive origin shattered on the stone floor next to it. Down the steps in the sitting area, I could see more furniture knocked over, dirt and spilled orchids on the carpet, pictures askew on the wall—or knocked down altogether. I couldn't see the kitchen from where I stood, but the number of dishes on the hall floor—broken and whole—implied it was as ransacked as the rest.

"You have to call the police," JoJo said. "This isn't just some little break-and-enter. This is serious vandalism…and probably theft, even."

"Theft," Lisa whispered, suddenly steely and in-control. Her old self. "I need to know what they've taken." She put a firm hand out, grabbing JoJo's phone before he could dial. "Don't. Help me search." She turned back to me. "Thank you, Cam. But I think JoJo and I can handle this now."

"I…" I stammered, stunned at her abrupt dismissal. "You're sure nobody's here?" *And what would I do if there were?* I asked myself, feeling my skin tingle. *Disappear?*

"I'm sure," she said. "My apologies for frightening you, Cam. We'll talk soon." She practically pushed me out the door, closing it firmly in my face.

I stood on her porch a long moment before walking slowly back toward the Brixton estate. Toward my empty house, with its nineteen-pound lump of skin and flesh and bone. My own skin shivered, but I stayed visible.

I'd been so relieved this was over. And now, clearly, it was not.

∾

A shriek stopped me in my tracks halfway down the path between the estates. Lisa's shriek. I froze, my skin flaring into painful tingles, already half-chameleon.

There was no second shriek; I heard nothing else. Just the wind rustling through the trees, and, in the distance, the low horn of a ferry. *Mom?* I thought, but no, it had to just be an inter-island boat. Mom and Dad wouldn't be here till close to eight.

Still silence from Lisa's. My skin settled down, and I could see my arms again.

Just go home, Cam, I told myself. *It was nothing.* Maybe she and JoJo were teasing each other. Maybe they were… Nah. I didn't want to think about it, whatever it was.

But maybe it was a real shriek. Maybe they were both in danger.

How would I feel if I walked away when I could have helped? But how much had I actually helped anything in the last few weeks? My presence seemed to attract danger and strangeness. No, I'd let them handle this without my bumbling efforts to help.

Except, of course, if I'd learned one thing in my time on Orcas, it was the necessity of reaching out, of being connected. With a heavy sigh, I turned and walked back to Lisa's house.

I climbed the few steps to her front door slowly, my shoes making no noise at all. I stood at the door a minute, listening, and wishing this house had those little windows beside the door that some houses had. I could peer in and reassure myself and go away.

Though of course, Lisa would never expose herself to the world like that. Not even at the end of her driveway, behind her gate. She would be quiet and composed and private and alone.

I heard nothing, and I kept hearing nothing. So, eventually, steeling my resolve and making sure my skin was calm, I knocked.

No one answered. Well, it had been a kind of soft knock. I tried again, louder this time.

After another long minute, I heard footsteps. Then the door slowly opened, and JoJo peered out. He opened the door all the way and stepped back. "You might as well come in."

"I heard a—" I started, but he was already walking away from me.

I shut the door behind me and followed him, stepping around the toppled entry table, avoiding the broken pottery. When we reached the sunken living room, I again tried to say something, but stopped abruptly as two facts become horribly clear:

Lisa Cannon was crumpled in a chair, quietly sobbing.

And there was a body sprawled next to the coffee table. A dead body.

CHAPTER 2

Fortunately, JoJo went right back to attending to Lisa, so I was able to vanish and then reappear without him noticing. Efficient, and much faster than usual. *Gee, I'm getting kind of good at this*, I told myself. It's what I do, when I'm startled or panicked: I disappear. Literally, actually; people find it pretty much impossible to see me, or even remember that I was there. A very useful trait when you're the smallest, least powerful person in the room. A gigantic, awkward pain in the ass, when you're an adult trying to live in the real world. If I could cure myself of my supernatural disability, I would in a heartbeat. Even if it had saved my life just the week before.

I gripped the back of the sofa, grounding myself, coming back into full view. When I was sure I had it under control, I took a deep breath and forced myself to look at the body on the floor.

It was a man, facedown, legs slightly splayed, one arm bent under his body at an unnatural angle. One hand clutched a pillowcase full of—whatever he'd been stealing, I guessed. Grizzled grey hair spread in a mop around his head, reaching several feet in every direction; his filthy blue jeans and canvas jacket were probably staining Lisa's priceless carpet. I didn't see any blood, but that didn't mean he wasn't covering up a pool of it.

It was so obvious this man was dead. I felt a tingle, but I knew there was no threat.

I shivered, diverting my gaze, and walked across the room. Lisa was sniffling once more, and JoJo was soothing her. Just like back at my place, ten minutes ago.

"Who...who is that guy?" I stammered. "What happened?"

Lisa blinked up at me, shivering as she looked over JoJo's shoulder. "I have no earthly idea," she said in a husky whisper. "I just... we were looking for...I almost tripped over him."

JoJo sat down on the floor next to Lisa's chair, keeping a hand on her knee as he looked over at the body. "Looks like a boat dude, if you ask me."

"Boat dude?" I echoed.

Lisa was once again collecting herself. I wondered how many times in a row she could fall apart and put herself back together without suffering whiplash. "It's an island thing, Cam dear," she said. "City homeless are street people; ours are boat dudes."

I glanced back at the body. Yes, he looked pretty ragged, and he'd filled that pillowcase with something. "But if he had a boat to live on, then was he homeless?"

JoJo gave a sort of strangled laugh. "Okay, he's not homeless, whatever." He turned back to Lisa; his voice rose as he said, "So Lisa, can we call 911 *now*?" Maybe they were just handing the panic back and forth between them. A sort of collaborative thing.

She sighed and got to her feet. "I imagine we must." But she only strode over to the tall windows and looked down at the water below.

"I...I can do it," I stammered, pulling out my cell phone, hoping my signal would be there. I never knew on this island.

"Wait," she said, wheeling about. "Just call Kip. No need for 911." She waved a disdainful hand at the body. "There's no emergency here—this person has been dead for an hour at least."

"How do you know?" asked JoJo, his voice approaching a whine.

"Because...well, just look at him."

I shivered again. "I'd rather not."

Fortunately, or not, Kip's direct line was programmed into my phone. Though even that was unnecessary; it was easy to find in my recent calls. When the local sheriff's deputy accounts for almost half the phone calls you make, it seems like maybe a good time to question your life choices.

"Cam?" came the deputy's mellifluous voice over the line. I felt a blush creeping up my cheeks and turned so the others wouldn't see. "Need turkey-cooking advice?"

"Oh, Kip. I'm at Lisa's. You've got to come. Quick."

"What is it?" His voice was instantly serious. "Are you all right?"

"Yes! Yes, I'm fine. But...this other guy isn't, so much."

"Who? Do we need an ambulance?"

"No, I mean, I don't think so. Just come over here!" I hung up the phone before I started sounding as hysterical as JoJo. Or Lisa, depending on whoever's turn it was this minute.

It rang again immediately: Kip. "Cam, I'm on my way, but you've got to give me more information than that. Is anyone in danger? Do I need to bring backup?"

"No—there was an intruder at Lisa's, and—well, he's dead. We have a dead burglar here. You have to come!"

"A dead burglar? Did someone shoot him?"

"No!" I closed my eyes and composed myself. "No. It looks like he just...died here."

"Well, we need to confirm that. All right, all right." In the background, I could hear the sound of the engine; so he was on his way. Good. "I'll be there in ten minutes. Don't touch anything."

I rolled my eyes. "I know *that*." I'd learned that lesson last week, too.

After I hung up the second time, Lisa stepped over to the body. She seemed entirely calm and collected once more, which in turn helped me calm down.

"He said not to touch anything," I told her.

She gave me the same look I'd just given Kip (even if he hadn't seen it), though she looked like a million bucks doing it, not like the sulky-teenager pouty-face I was sure I had managed. "No, of course not. I'm just trying to figure out who it is. From the clothes, it could be any number of folks, but from the hair, I'm thinking it might be Snooks."

"You think?" JoJo asked, also coming over to peer down at the body.

"Snooks?" I asked.

"Ephraim Snooks," JoJo said, nodding at Lisa. "Yeah, could be." He turned back to me. "He lives on his boat down past Deer Harbor, and sometimes shuttles folks over to Crane Island for a few bucks."

I knew that everyone knew everyone on Orcas Island, but I hadn't realized that that extended to the homeless population. "Why was he robbing Lisa's house? What's in that pillowcase?"

"That's the question, isn't it," Lisa said. "I suppose he wanted drugs, some leftover Vicodin or whatever he could find in the medicine cabinet." She watched me glance around the ransacked living room. "Yes, I know, he certainly did a lot of damage if he just wanted painkillers. Broke in here, trashed my house and fell over dead."

"Hm." I thought a moment. "Did he hate you?"

She shrugged. "Not that I know of. But he never was all that stable."

"If indeed this is him," JoJo put in.

"If indeed." We all stared at the body another minute. I don't know about the rest of them, but I was super glad we were not supposed to touch anything.

Lisa straightened and put on her crisp, professional smile. "Well! Shall we wait in the dining room, perhaps, for Deputy Rankin? I'm finding it a little…morbid in here."

"Brilliant," JoJo said, in a slight English accent. Was he being…*funny*?

We went down a hall to her formal dining room—another of the many rooms in her house I had never seen before, and one that was only a little bit ransacked. It too had an expansive view of the little cove below, but from a slightly different angle, as it was off the far side of the kitchen, further along the great arcing sweep of her house. Weirdly, there was a bottle of wine already open on a mahogany sideboard, next to a half-dozen sparkling-clean wine glasses. "JoJo, would you mind?" she asked, picking up an overturned chair and setting it right.

"Of course not." He poured three glasses and handed them around.

Lisa nodded at the long table. "Have a seat." She straightened a massive centerpiece (were those actual live orchids built into it?) and sat down at the head of the table. JoJo sat to her right, so I took the chair to her left.

"Ow," I said, immediately popping back up. "What the—"

"What is it?" Lisa asked, frowning.

I looked at the opulently embroidered seat of the chair, then reached down and picked up a small, open binder. "This."

She took the binder and began to laugh. "Oh. My apologies. It's Bella's script. She's incorrigible."

"Bella?"

"One of my actors. I keep forgetting that you don't really know them, which you should, since they'll be presenting your work this summer." She shook her head. "We've just started blocking for *Stranger Times*, the next play after *Murder for Two,* and she's the lead. An important early scene takes place in a dining room, so I said they should work in here." She tossed the binder on the table. "I'll ask her to be more careful in the future."

I sipped my wine. It was, no surprise, amazingly delicious. I took another sip before setting it on the table and glancing surreptitiously at the time on my phone. It was already nearly five, and I had a long evening ahead of me: my parents would be here a little before eight, and I hadn't gotten dinner started yet. Not to mention getting that turkey brined.

How could I be thinking about my turkey when there was a dead guy on the floor in the next room? Had my life really gotten that absurd, or was there only so much capacity in the human brain for this sort of thing, before it just went *tilt* and insisted on returning to the mundane?

JoJo took a healthy swig of his wine, seeming not to notice the taste at all, and was about to say something when there was a commotion from the front hall. A spike of fear shot through me even as Lisa got to her feet.

"Oh my goodness, the troupe is back already," she said. "That's just what we need."

Cries of surprise and alarm wafted in from the front hall as Lisa left the room. "I know, I know!" I heard her say. "The authorities are on their way—no, don't go down there!"

JoJo smirked at me and raised his glass. "Lisa says she never wanted children, so she went and adopted a dozen actors."

"She does seem to love working with them, and having them stay here."

"It gives her something to complain about. So you have a play, and it's on the docket? I never knew you were a playwright, Camille Tate. A woman of many mysteries."

I was almost blushing. "It's coming along." I'd been able to devote myself to the play during my recovery, as Jen came by every day to check on the Brixton place and encourage me. I still had trouble believing Lisa wanted it for the summer season, but she insisted that she did.

"I always wanted to write a screenplay, myself," JoJo said.

"Well, that's what I thought I was doing, but Lisa thinks this would work for the stage. And I'm really excited about it."

"What's it about?"

"It's, um, kind of a mystery. Involving a hairdresser. And a bunch of her wacky customers. Actually it's taking a different direction than where I first thought it was going."

"Fascinating. Where do you get your ideas?" he asked.

"From the ether." I shrugged. I hated talking about myself. I decided to change the subject, and maybe figure out what the deal was between him and Lisa. "So…you and Lisa seem to know each other pretty well?"

JoJo merely raised an eyebrow and nodded. "Indeed."

"What with being neighbors and all, I guess," I added. *Oh, so smooth, Cam.*

"Indeed again."

My subtle fishing expedition was obviously not subtle enough.

I retreated from this exquisitely awkward line of conversation and went back to my wine as we both listened to the conversation in the front hall, though we couldn't hear anything of what was actually being said. After another minute, Lisa came back in. "I've sent them to the guesthouse for now. Where is that darn—?"

A sharp knock on the door interrupted her. Kip, at last.

❧

Five minutes later, we were all back in the living room, watching San Juan County Deputy Sheriff Kip Rankin stare down at a dead body on the carpet. I found myself missing my wine; JoJo had brought his glass, which he had nearly finished.

Kip pulled on blue rubber medical gloves. He briefly held the wrist of whoever it was, then put two fingers deep into a grizzled white beard, feeling for a pulse. He shook his head and consulted his watch. "Normally this is the coroner's job, but it's clear what we're dealing with, here. Well," said Kip, turning to Lisa and me. "You ladies do seem to attract such interesting…company."

"Now Kip—" Lisa started, but he gave her a smile and a placating wave of his hands.

"There's no need to get your feathers ruffled, Lisa. I'll be taking a few pictures, and then I plan to roll him over and attempt an identification. Perhaps you'd be more comfortable in the other room?"

"I'm staying right here," Lisa said, straightening her spine.

I swallowed. I could stay here, or I could go back to that nice dining room, with that nice view of the water below, and that nice glass of wine…

But then Kip had somehow already snapped the pictures he wanted, and was rolling the guy over. The body landed on its back with a quiet thud.

"Ephraim Snooks," JoJo said, and raised his glass to the corpse.

Lisa just nodded, her face pale.

Kip was murmuring into a little radio handset, numbers and cop code, but it sounded as though he concurred.

I made myself look at the dude's face, and then down his front. There wasn't a mark on him. "There's no blood. How did he die?" I asked.

Kip raised an eyebrow at me. He almost looked pleased. He flipped a switch on his radio and returned it to his belt. "That is the question of the hour, Camille. I'll be looking to you-all for those answers."

Lisa gave him a weary smile. "I don't suppose you'd take a glass of wine?"

"I'm on duty, Lisa." And somehow, he smiled.

❧

He questioned us all separately, starting with me. We sat in the dining room, and he didn't have any wine, so I felt a little awkward drinking mine, though not awkward enough not to do so. I was determined not to vanish. I told him what I knew, which was basically nothing. Lisa had come home, found her house ransacked, thought she saw an intruder, rushed to my place. We'd come over, they'd found the body, we called Kip. She and JoJo knew who the guy was, but had no clue why he was here.

"Is anything missing?"

I frowned. "I guess whatever's in that pillowcase. You probably want to ask Lisa." Kip looked up at me, a bit sharply, like he was wondering if I was being sarcastic. "I mean, of course I don't know!" I went on. "She said she just ran over to my place, she didn't look around. She seemed worried about it. Which is normal, right? If someone breaks into your house and looks for things, maybe you wonder what he's looking for?" Great, now I was babbling. Chameleoning wouldn't be far behind.

"All right, Cam, we'll take a look then," Kip said, closing his notebook and turning off the tape recorder. "You can go now."

"But—wait, really? Is that all?" I was actually curious about the contents of the pillowcase. I realized that I, too, was looking for clues.

He gave me a gentle smile. "Of course not, but that's all I need from you right now. Don't you have Thanksgiving preparations to make?"

"Oh!" I pulled out my phone and looked at the time again. Almost six-thirty. "Oh, my parents are going to be here in an hour! I haven't even started dinner."

"You don't need me to walk you home, do you?"

"No, gosh, no." I got to my feet. "The intruder seems…not very dangerous any more."

Kip's smile grew. "No, he's probably not going to bother you. Assuming he was working alone, that is."

"What?"

"Which is what I am assuming!" he hastened to add, as he got up as well. "I'll see you to the door at least."

"Thanks."

❧

True to his word, Kip escorted me to Lisa's front door and shut it behind me. I barely had a chance to wave at Lisa and JoJo on my way out. Was he really that interested in us not talking to each other?

No, probably not, I decided. He'd left them alone together the whole time he'd been questioning me, after all. Not to mention the ten or whatever minutes it had taken him to get here in the first place.

This time, my trip down the path back to the Brixton estate

was uneventful. It was my arrival that was different.

The sun had set while I was at Lisa's, and the Brixtons' main house blazed with lights on all three floors. A sleek grey Mercedes and a red Tesla were parked out front; matching brown luggage with signature gold patterns on it sat all around the open trunk of the Mercedes.

Diana and Emmett Brixton had obviously arrived.

"Oh!" I gasped. I took a moment to assess my skin—these were my employers, I'd been expecting them, there was nothing to be frightened of, everything was *fine* and I'd had a glass of *wine*—and walked up to the front door. But I was supposed to be caretaking, and as part of that, I needed to let them know about the break-in next door, didn't I?

I did.

After another moment of hesitation while I pondered whether a caretaker rings the doorbell or just walks in, I rang it. After a pause long enough to make me wonder if I should ring it again or just go back to my guesthouse, the door opened. A woman in her mid-thirties with an absolutely perfect Louise Brooks bob stood there. She had clearly taken the time to work on her pose as well, cocking a hip and peering at me from under heavy bangs. She was sporting a slim black dress, a long string of pearls, and red lipstick. Though I knew from photos that she had the same sandy-blond hair as her brother, Clary Brixton had completed the look with an expensive dye job. She looked like the kind of vampire you'd gladly throw yourself at, and I don't even like girls that way.

"Yes?" she purred.

I put out my hand. "I'm Cam Tate. The caretaker."

She looked down at my hand as though she expected to find leaflets for a particularly dull community meeting there, before finally taking it and giving it a limp shake. "Oh yes. Of course. I'm Clary." She did not move out of the doorway.

Yes, I know, I didn't say. "Um, I just wanted to let your folks know I'm here, and see if they need anything? And I need to tell them that…"

"I think we're fine. Thank you."

She closed the door on me.

Well, that was nice. I stood there a minute longer, wondering if I should try again, or call Diana, or what. I had no confidence Clary would actually convey the message. *No, they'll figure it out when they see the guesthouse lights on*, I told myself, and went home.

The guesthouse was freezing: somehow, I'd left the kitchen door open when we'd rushed over to Lisa's. The turkey still sat on the counter. "Oh no!" I touched it, but it was as chilly as when it had come out of the fridge. Well, that made sense: it was cold as a meat locker in here. I guess if you're going to leave a giant hunk of raw poultry out for a few hours, late November in the Pacific Northwest is a good time to do so.

How could I have left the door open? Had we been *that* distracted? Now, of all times? No, I couldn't have.

Heart pounding, skin a roil of prickles and pain, I ran through the house, looking for signs of an intruder, but found none. Everything was just as I had left it. I returned slowly to the kitchen, trying to settle down yet again. How many frights in one day could a body handle? I must be getting to my limit by now. I wanted to vanish and I wanted not to vanish. But I'd had wine.

I made myself breathe deeply.

Maybe my stupid cat had opened the door. I wouldn't put it past him. I inspected the turkey more carefully but didn't see any signs of gnawing or other feline misadventure. "James!" I called, cruising through the house again. He was nowhere.

It was almost seven by now. My house was freezing and I hadn't started dinner and my folks were going to be here soon. And, yeah, I still had this giant hunk of raw poultry out on my kitchen counter.

"I just won't brine it," I said to myself. I didn't have a big enough pot anyway. Ironic, I thought: here I was on an island surrounded by frigid salt water, and I couldn't find a way to put a nineteen-pound turkey into frigid salt water.

I went to the front room and jacked up the heat, wishing I had time to build a fire—I hadn't laid one earlier, it had been such a pleasant day. Well, maybe Dad would want to. Be useful and manly and all that. Just the sort of thing he'd like.

Back in the kitchen, I wrestled the turkey back into the fridge, where it took up the entire bottom shelf. It was tempting just to leave it outside all night, but even a city girl like me knew that would be dumb.

"James!" I called out the back door. The orange fluffbutt didn't show. "Fine, be that way," I muttered, and got out a pan that would do fine for lasagna. I thought.

I had just opened the recipe book when there was a knock on the front door. "Cripes!" How could they have gotten here so fast? It wasn't even seven-thirty—had the ferry been early? Had they driven from the ferry landing at ninety miles an hour? I rushed to the door, only to find Jen Darling there, her unmarked white van parked on the gravel drive. Her cheeks were pink from the chill outside; her red corkscrew curls bounced and her eyes were bright.

"Brr! Why don't you light a fire?" she said, brushing past me on her way in.

"I don't have time! I've been…oh, you wouldn't believe it. What are you doing here?" I asked, shutting the door behind her.

"I heard about the latest murder in town! I came to see if you're all right."

I gaped at her. "Um, it—wasn't a murder." Wasn't it? "Just a dead guy in Lisa Cannon's house."

"I know! Snooks, keeling over in the middle of a burglary! I didn't know he was like that." Her eyes were wide, and, as usual, she was way too excited about this. Not scared or disturbed or anything normal. She should be disturbed, we should all be disturbed. People dropping dead right and left: this was disturbing. But Jen *loved* the intrigue. "Did you see the body?"

"I did, and Kip is already there, and—how did you even get in here? You didn't buzz the gate."

She rubbed her hands together and knelt down in front of the fireplace. "Well, if you're not going to, I will." As she crumpled up newspaper and laid kindling, she added, "The Brixtons usually leave the gate open when they're here."

"Oh." That seemed kind of unlike them, particularly Diana, and it hadn't been covered in the inch-thick house manual, but okay, good to know.

My cell phone rang even as I heard tires crunching on the gravel. "It's my folks!" I said as I pulled the phone out of my pocket. "Jen, can you get the door?"

But it was Mom's number on the screen. I swiped the call open. "Mom?"

"Oh, honey! I'm so sorry! We missed the ferry."

Jen opened the door and Colin walked in. I gaped at him and said into the phone, "What? You already told me that."

"No, hon, we missed the next one too."

"How did you *do* that?"

Mom gave a rueful chuckle. "Well, it was like three hours between them, and your dad didn't want to wait at the ferry landing all that time. They have a lousy snack bar, nothing but stale pastries and overpriced ice cream. And it was cold. So we went into town to get something to eat, and, well, apparently you're supposed to be here thirty minutes early or something."

"Mom!" I tried not to wail. "I told you all that! And I'm cooking you dinner!"

"Oh, no need for that—we're full up. Found the best burgers on the West Coast."

I pulled the phone away from my head briefly so she wouldn't hear my exasperated sigh, then put it back. "So, when are you getting here now? *Is* there another ferry?"

"Cook *us* dinner," Colin said, giving me a wolfish grin. "I'm starved."

Shut up, I mouthed to him, and turned my back so I couldn't see him.

Mom said, "The last one of the night leaves at eight fifty-five, gets to the island at nine fifty-five. We'll be on it, I promise."

Great. Now they wouldn't be here till bedtime. "Okay," I told her. "Just—keep your car in the line, and don't get out of it. Don't even go to the snack bar. Or the bathroom. Seriously."

"Cam, love, I'm sorry."

"And don't drain your battery running the heater and the radio. Leave the car on."

She laughed. "We'll see you soon."

I stuffed the phone in my pocket and turned back to my friends. "Who wants lasagna?"

"I'm always hungry, but I came over to see if you're okay," Colin said. "Is it true you found Snooks dead at Lisa Cannon's house?"

"Does everyone here know everything that happens?"

Jan and Colin traded looks, then both nodded in unison.

"Fine. I'll tell you about it after we cook."

❦

Jen got the fire roaring while Colin helped me with the spices for the lasagna. In fact, he had so many ideas about how to improve the (admittedly rather bland-looking) recipe I'd found, I eventually just sat back and let him work.

Then we settled in the cozy living room with beers while the food baked. "You okay, though?" Colin's concern was obvious, even though he was trying to be casual. "You've been through enough, Cam."

Jen was also watching me, which made me embarrassed. "I'm glad your parents will be here this weekend."

"If they ever get here. My parents are so clueless," I said, staring gloomily into the fire.

"All parents are," Jen agreed, and Colin raised his bottle.

"I was hoping she'd help me get the meal for tomorrow set up."
I took a swig of my beer. "I have no idea what I'm doing here.
Does turkey really have to be brined?"

Colin shrugged. "Nah. It'll be great, whatever you do. I can
stop by in the morning and give you a hand if you like."

I stared back at him as a sudden thought struck me. "Wait,
where are you having Thanksgiving dinner? You too, Jen?"

Jen laughed. "I'm good—going to Katrina's house." Katrina
was her boss at the Barnacle Bar. "She gives a big potluck shindig
every year. I wouldn't miss it." She gave me a sly grin. "I saved
back a batch of zucchini muffins in the freezer. I'm taking those."

"What about you?" I turned to Colin.

He gave an all-too-casual shrug. "Don't worry about me. I'll
rustle something up."

"You will not!" I practically shouted. "You'll come here. There's
plenty of food. And you'll love my clueless parents."

His gaze softened as he looked back at me. He was obviously
touched, and trying to be cool about it. "Well, um, sure. If it's
not an imposition…"

"Not at all!" Out of the corner of my eye, I could see Jen
watching us avidly. Still trying to play matchmaker, no doubt.
Even though she knew I was only interested in Colin as a *friend*.
She was his friend, had been for years; she of all people should
understand that men and women could be *friends*. "And I will totally take you up on the offer for help. I've never done this before.
I can barely make ramen. I bought a nineteen-pound turkey."

Both Colin and Jen busted out laughing at this. "For how
many people?" Jen asked.

I shrugged, staring at the fire. "Um. Me and my folks. And
now Colin."

"Well, plenty of leftovers," Colin said.

"Exactly! Turkey sandwiches!"

"So," Colin said, after a short pause. "About this latest murder."

"It wasn't a murder!" I said, again.

"Yeah," Jen put in, her voice heavy with irony. "Just a mysteriously dead body at Lisa Cannon's house."

"How do these things get out?" I asked. "Does the whole island know?"

"Word gets around," Colin said.

"I guess so." I sipped my beer. "Remind me never to murder anyone. Although that wasn't murder."

"What was it?"

"I don't know. Just a guy who dropped dead. A guy who lives on his boat." My face flushed as I said that, remembering where Colin currently lived. "I mean, um, sort of permanently, I guess." Of course I was only making it worse. Snooks wasn't living anywhere, now.

Colin shook his head. "Ephraim was all right, for a boat dude."

"How was he killed?" Jen asked.

I gave her a helpless look. "Honest to god, I don't know. He was just…dead, lying in her living room. No blood or anything like that. I think it was a burglary."

"A burglary? Doesn't sound like Ephraim." Colin was frowning.

Jen shook her head. "That's what I thought."

I wondered what else to tell them. Or was I not supposed to tell them anything? Since word was already all over the island anyway, what could it hurt? Besides, Kip hadn't asked me to keep anything quiet. "Her place was ransacked, and there was a pillowcase full of something in his hand."

"Wow." Jen shook her head and took a healthy swig of her beer. "Ephraim Snooks, secret burglar. What's going on with our sleepy little island?" She and Colin exchanged a glance. "If this keeps up, we might as well all move to Seattle."

"Might as well."

I actually felt guilty. Like I'd brought this mess with me.

We drank in silence another few minutes, until good smells

started emanating from the kitchen. I got up and went to check on the lasagna. It was bubbling nicely, but clearly still needed a little longer. I took the opportunity to call for James again out the back door, but he still didn't show. Oh well. He had his fur coat on. He'd show up when he got hungry enough.

Colin appeared at the kitchen doorway. "Time to make a salad?"

"You're just trying to make yourself indispensible."

He nodded, touching the bill of his cap with his beer bottle. "Got me figured."

Jen came in as well, and between the three of us, we had a big green salad made and the table set by the time the lasagna was ready. Colin pulled it out of the oven with a flourish and set it on top of the stove. "Let it cool a few," he said. "We can start on the salad."

As we ate, I looked around the table at my friends. Okay, it wasn't the vision I'd had for this evening—and when would I learn that nothing ever went as planned, anyway?—but here were people who cared about me, sharing a delicious home-cooked meal at a convivial table, and that was pretty darn good.

CHAPTER 3

After dinner, Colin helped me clean up while Jen stoked the fire. "Gotta get the place nice and cozy for your clueless folks!" she called cheerfully from the living room.

I pulled out my phone to check the time. Nine-thirty; they should be landing in a half hour. "You guys want to meet them?" I called back.

"Nah, I gotta get home. Maybe later on the weekend?"

"Sure."

She came back in, rubbing sooty hands on her jeans. "You two all good here?"

"Yep." I glanced around the kitchen. "Practically done."

Colin indicated the half-empty lasagna pan on the stove. "Got foil for this?"

"I do, but I don't think I have room in the fridge." I went over and opened it. The turkey reclined on the bottom shelf; cream and milk and soda and beer and cider crammed the top shelf; the shelves in between were a jumble of greens, butter, olives, carrots, bagels, eggs, four kinds of cheese, two kinds of sandwich bread, mayonnaise and mustard and capers, not to mention two pies (cherry and pumpkin). I was planning to make a Jello salad too, for the sake of family tradition, but that could be tomorrow. "Maybe if we squeezed it into a smaller container?"

"Maybe your parents will be hungry," Jen mused, staring at the mountain of food. You couldn't even see the back of the fridge. "No problem leaving it out till they get here, at least."

"Yeah. Good idea."

"Well, I gotta jet," she said, heading back out to the living room for her jacket.

Colin lingered behind, looking shy and even more adorable than usual. "So...should I meet them now, or wait till tomorrow?"

Ah, yes, of course...if he was here tonight, and Jen was gone, *and* they learned I'd invited him to Thanksgiving dinner... "Maybe tomorrow is better. I can tell them you're coming, and who you are, and all."

"Right. Got it." He marched out to the front room and pulled his own jacket on. Out front, I heard Jen's truck start up and pull out. "So—what time tomorrow?"

I thought a moment. "We're eating at four, so the turkey should go in around—" Oh crap, I hadn't even figured that out yet.

Colin smiled. "Gonna stuff it?"

"I...thought I would?"

"Then say five hours, maybe a little less."

"Okay, so eleven."

Now he laughed, though still in a kindly sort of way. "No, no, no. If dinner's at four, turkey has to come out by three anyway. Time to get the stuffing out, let the bird rest, make the gravy. So it goes in by ten, ten-thirty. You really haven't done this before, have you?"

I shrugged, feeling defensive. "I've helped my mom." *And my ex-boyfriend was the world's biggest foodie and never even let me in the kitchen...*

Colin put a gentle hand on my shoulder. "Don't worry. It's gonna be fine. I'll get here at nine-thirty, help get it stuffed and in."

I grabbed him in a sudden hug, holding him fiercely tight.

"Oh, Colin, thank you!"

He hugged me back, releasing me after a minute. "Gotta get out of here so we don't get caught like this." He gently laid his hand over my bandage, which was hidden by my shirt. "Gotta watch out for you, Cam. Make sure you don't overdo it."

This whole friendship thing. It was amazing. I smiled and let him go. "Drive safe. See you tomorrow!"

His red pickup rattled back up the driveway, around the main house, and up to the road. I touched my bandage, pressing just lightly enough to feel the sting of the stitches.

I spared a moment to wonder what was going on up in the big house, and if they were wondering what was going on back here with all these cars coming and going. I needed to let Diana know about that burglary, too.

But first, I needed to locate my wayward kitten. "James!" I called into the night. "James, kitty kitty! Time to come in!" Nothing. "I'll give you some lasagna!" Nothing.

I shut the door before all the fire-heat could escape, and sat down to try calling the Brixtons.

No answer.

All I had to do was wait for my clueless parents.

ஒ

Soon enough, a familiar green Lexus was pulling up in front of the guesthouse, and car and trunk doors were slamming, and here came my folks. All this way to visit me. I felt my eyes filling with sentimental tears as I rushed outside to hug them, and help them bring their luggage in. Although Dad wouldn't let me, of course.

"Not a chance! I've got it all, see?" He grinned, showing me how he was easily holding three duffel bags and Mom's toiletries kit, with an extra pillow under one long, ropey arm. He looked up at the guesthouse, and back at the main house beyond. "Jeez, hon, you've really hit a home run with this place, haven't you?"

"Don't be silly, Adam, she hasn't bought it," Mom said gently. "It's just a job."

"Well, that's what I meant!"

Mom was pulling me into a fierce hug, as Dad's arms were full. "Come on inside, you guys," I said. "Are you sure I can't carry anything?"

"Not a thing!"

I showed them to their room, where Mom cooed over how adorable it was and Dad dumped everything on the bed before heading back outside for a second load, the big fibber.

"There's more luggage?"

"Just some car snacks!"

"Honey, it's so great to see you." Mom sat down on the bed and patted the place beside her. I sat down and snuggled close as she put an arm around me. "I'm sorry we missed dinner."

"That's all right. I had some friends over." Then, realizing now was as good a time as any, I went on: "In fact, I invited one of them to come to Thanksgiving dinner tomorrow—Colin. He's one of the ones who saved me...last week."

She squeezed me even tighter, her arm brushing close to my bandage. I winced and moved. I'd told them about the kidnaping, but I'd left out the part where I got shot. There is no good way to tell your parents that you've been shot.

"I still can't believe you fell into such a nest of intrigue!" she said. "Thank goodness it's over."

"Mm-hmm," I murmured. Because it was over, of course it was. Gunshot wounds and dead bodies at Lisa's house notwithstanding.

"And we'll be delighted to meet your new *friend*," she went on.

"Mom. Friend is the operative word."

"Mm-hmm."

Dad came back in with four grocery bags stuffed with food. "Kitchen there?" He nodded toward the back of the house.

"Dad!" I got up and tried to take one of the bags away, but he was having none of it. "This way." He followed me down the hall.

"What is all this?" I asked, as he set the groceries on the table. "I told you guys I had everything!"

"Your mom wanted to pick up a few things," he said, grinning at my mom in the doorway. "She didn't believe you'd remember it all. I told her…"

"Adam," my mom chided, still smiling.

"Well, it's always good to have a deep bullpen," he muttered.

I opened the fridge, stared inside, and shut it again. "I don't know where we're going to put everything." And the half-pan of lasagna still sat on the stove.

"It's cold enough outside!" Dad said. "Just set it out the back door there?"

"Well, um…"

He frowned at the door. "You got wild animals here? Of course you don't, it's an island."

"Bears can swim," my mom said.

"I don't think we have bears here," I said, "but I've seen tons of deer. And there's rabbits, and probably raccoons. And river otters. Don't put any meat or vegetables outside." *And there's my cat too,* I thought. But he'd be in by bedtime, right?

Mom started unpacking the grocery bags. Dinner rolls, about ten pounds of sweet potatoes, a box of oatmeal cookies, two more pounds of butter, Martinelli's sparkling cider, a string bag of oranges… One of the bags had nothing but bottles of wine. "Jeez, you guys," I said.

"You said the island's grocery store was expensive," my mom said, unfazed.

"Not *that* expensive. We could eat for weeks on this—you guys are only here till Saturday, right?"

"Saturday *afternoon*," Dad said, and Mom added, "That's days from now, and it's a holiday where we give thanks for our bounty. You'll want all this. Just keep what we don't eat this weekend."

"Well, we'll see what we can do." I gathered up the sweet potatoes and the bag of dinner rolls and opened the back door. Or tried to, anyway; something was leaning against it. I pushed the door gently, nudging whatever-it-was forward.

"Oh, how marvelous!" Mom said, looking over my shoulder. "We can make zucchini bread!"

I clutched the door, struggling with keeping my skin calm, and more or less succeeding. There, leaning against the side of the house just beside the door, was not one but four enormous zucchini.

Mom pushed past me and gathered the absurd vegetables up, looking them over, brushing off bits of dirt from the biggest one. "How charming! You must have such great neighbors here." Then she saw my expression. "What's the matter? What is it?"

"Your mom makes excellent zucchini bread," Dad put in, unnecessarily. "Out of the park every time."

"I…" I stammered, trying to make sense of it. "I…thought the neighbor who was doing this had…left." I went out onto the porch and looked around. Nobody. I stepped further into the yard, my mind reeling. Sheila was dead! Wasn't she? She had to be.

But they haven't found the body, a little voice in my head reminded me. *They just presumed she was dead…there was blood, sure, but no body.*

Had she broken into Lisa's house too?

But then, what about the boat dude?

And why would she leave me more squash? Was it a gift or…a warning?

"Honey?" Mom called, from the back door.

"James! Here, kitty kitty! Here, James!" I called out, stepping further into the night as my fear spiked even higher. Where was my *cat*? Had she taken him? "James!!" But, she'd given me the cat. She'd protected and fed him, then gave him to me for safekeeping. Surely she wouldn't take him or hurt him?

She's a madwoman, I thought. *Who can say what she'd do?*

"She's calling her cat," I heard Mom tell Dad.

"She has a cat?"

I stayed in the dark till I was sure I was entirely visible once more. I knew I had vanished in front of my parents, many times—particularly when they'd first taken me in, before I'd even really understood what was different about me. I'd known that I was safer when my skin felt this way, and I'd also understood that whatever was happening to me was very, very unusual. No one else I knew was erased from their surroundings when they were frightened. I was wrong, strange, different, a freak. So we never talked about it, and I'd kept it from them as best I could.

At least my foster parents had cared enough to wonder where I'd gotten to when I vanished. They would explain it to themselves by saying I needed "time alone" when I was stressed, that I needed to go "hide" in my room, sometimes at a moment's notice. If they ever knew that it was something fundamentally supernatural, they never brought it up—with me, anyway, and probably not at all. I'm sure they were no more prepared to talk about it than I had ever been.

James didn't appear. I managed to tamp my fears and worries down into a tiny, manageable little ball of anxiety in the pit of my stomach, and went back inside.

Dad had opened a bottle of wine. I took the glass he handed me without protest, despite the late hour.

"Thanks, Dad."

He raised his own glass and clinked it against mine. "Any time."

We sipped, and my skin finished settling down. Even the belly-anxiety relaxed a bit. "Let's get as much of this put away as possible," I said, pulling more of the groceries out of the bags.

"Sure thing, coach."

"Adam?" Mom called from the hall bathroom. "Did you bring toothpaste?"

❦

We got settled into bed by about eleven-thirty. Not bad, considering. I heard them murmur to one another a bit, and then, a few minutes later, the familiar sound of my father's snores. Mom slept with earplugs. It was the only way they'd been able to stay married all these years.

It was so nice to have people in the house. They cared; they were taking care of me as best they could. I felt that same ease and safety that I'd felt when they first took me in. It had seemed like a miracle at the time, and after all these years, it still felt like that.

Exhausted though I was, it took me a long time to fall asleep. James hadn't spent every night in my bed with me, but he'd been here more often than not, especially on the colder nights. Each week in a kitten's life is years in a human life, and he was growing into an independent, leggy roamer. I knew he was an inquisitive and independent soul. He was shy with newcomers, so all the activity around the estate had probably put him off.

He didn't usually disappear for longer than a few hours, though; and I hadn't seen him since this afternoon. Had he wandered up to the road and been hit by a car? Was he sick with salmonella poisoning from licking that disgusting wrapper?

Had Sheila…?

No! I told myself. *Sheila is dead and James is fine, and if he's not, there's nothing you can do about it in the middle of the night.* If he was still missing tomorrow, I could go put up fliers in town. Assuming anything was open on Thanksgiving… No, he'd turn up. He always did.

More worrisome was the thought of the meal tomorrow, particularly if I did not get to sleep soon. Because I would wake up at five or five-thirty, like always, and there was a lot to do, a lot to keep track of.

Mom is here to help, I told myself. *And Colin will be here right after breakfast.* Heck, between the two of them, I could probably hang out with Dad and drink wine while they cooked.

Too bad it wasn't baseball season anymore.

Baseball figured in many of my fondest childhood memories, starting from way back when I was a terrified child, new to the household, who found some peace in sitting in front of the TV while Dad explained the infield fly rule, and why it was technically possible to have an unassisted triple play, though he'd only ever heard of it happening in Little League. In a pinch, I supposed, we could watch football. Thanksgiving Day involved plenty of football, I knew. But it wouldn't be the same. And did the TV even work here? I knew there was one hidden away in that big cherrywood cabinet in the living room. But I'd never turned it on. Brilliant screenwriters or playwrights (or whatever I was trying to be) didn't watch TV.

I would have sworn I was lying awake tossing and turning, but Mom's shriek woke me out of a deep, pillow-drooling slumber. I froze in bed, heart pounding.

"Get out! Get out!" I heard her yell, and then Dad's confused, muffled shouts after that.

An intruder! In here!

I forced myself to regain control of my limbs—*push, do it, breathe, there you go*—and pulled on my bathrobe. "Mom!" I called, when my voice could manage more than a croak. "Are you okay?"

"Argh!" she yelled. "Get out!"

"Lauren!" my dad hollered back at her. "Settle down!"

I rubbed my arms briskly as I dashed up the hall toward the guest bedroom, some faint part of my brain wondering why my dad was yelling at *her* and not the intruder. Their door was closed, but a strong light came from under it. Squinting a little against it, I opened the door.

James darted between my feet and streaked toward the front door. The flood of relief at seeing his dastardly little shape completely calmed me, and I wouldn't be disappearing.

"Get it out of here! Is it gone?" Mom was standing on the bed, clutching the bottom of her nightgown, trembling. "Did you see it?"

"Mom, it was my—"

"It was a huge rat! A huge rat *in the bed*!"

"Mom!" I yelled. "That was my cat! Now you've scared him!"

"Scared *him*!? What do you think he did to *me*?" Mom gave another shiver before flumping back down to sit on the bed. She clutched a pillow to herself and shook her head. "Cripes. I almost had a heart attack."

"You didn't tell us you had a cat," Dad said.

"You heard me calling for him!" I gaped at them. "You talked about it."

Mom and Dad exchanged an uncomfortable glance. "Um, yeah, I guess maybe we did," Dad said. "I guess maybe we forgot."

"I'm sorry, honey," Mom said. "I was fast asleep, and something warm and scrawny and furry brushed against my legs, and…"

"I'm sorry too," I said. "I don't know why he came in here, or how he even got back in the house. I've been looking for him since mid-afternoon. He ran out the back door."

"Why is he so small? I was sure it was a rat."

"He's a kitten. He's only half-grown. I just got him a few weeks ago."

"Cripes." She was calming down little by little. I could see it. I know what that looks like. How nice it must be, I thought for the millionth time, to just be able to freak out like a normal person.

"I'm sorry he scared you," I said again. "You going to be all right now?"

"Yes, hon." She leaned forward and gave me a hug. "I hope anyone can sleep, though!"

"Want me to make us all some cocoa?"

"I can do that," Dad said. He started to get up.

"No, no, let's just try sleeping," Mom said. "We're going to have enough calories tomorrow; we don't need a sugar hit in the middle of the night."

I snorted. "You're actually worried about calories on Thanksgiving?"

She laughed in return. "Well, I guess not. But still, the sugar wouldn't help me sleep."

"All right."

She settled back down into the bed. Dad shrugged and lay back beside her.

"Good night, again," I told them.

I got up and went out to the front room. James was sitting by the fireplace, giving me a look of insouciant disregard. "You little moron," I said, picking him up to carry back to my bed. "Where have you *been*?"

He did not illumine me.

Thursday

CHAPTER 4

Nor did my little jerk of a kitten get up early to make coffee and breakfast for everyone and stuff the nineteen-pound turkey.

"What good are you, anyway?" I asked him, as I ground fresh Local Goods Peruvian Dark beans, cringing a little at the noise of the grinder.

Unlike me, my parents were not early risers, even if we hadn't all been awakened at two a.m. with a feline crisis. But with Colin getting here at nine-thirty and the turkey going in by ten, seven was certainly late enough to get coffee going.

I tapped the grounds into the filter and filled the pot with cold water before pouring it into the machine and turning it on. Ahh, sweet relief was on its way.

I was slicing bagels and laying them on a baking sheet when Mom shuffled into the kitchen, rubbing her eyes. Her hair was sticking out all over the place, because she would not let me cut it into a style that was more bed-head friendly. "I still feel like I should be cutting *your* hair, little girl," she always said when I offered. "This is just too weird. Besides, Janice does a perfectly good job."

Janice doesn't ever see you in the mornings, I thought, but I just went and gave Mom a hug and said, "Did you guys ever get back to sleep?"

"Oh yes, after a little while."

"Good."

"Meow," said James, which I took to mean, *What are you doing with the coffee and bagels when you should be filling my bowl, and where's that giant piece of raw poultry that I thought was for me?*

"I guess he's a cute little guy," Mom said, reaching down to stroke him. James permitted it, clearly wondering if maybe *she* was going to feed him. "Why did you get a cat, though? Isn't this a temporary job? You can't have pets in your apartment in Seattle."

"Actually, I don't know how long this job is for—I think it can be long-term if I want it to be." I turned on the oven. "And that apartment in Seattle isn't mine. It's Kevin's." The coffee machine started to make those promising gurgling sounds, and a delightful aroma crept into the kitchen.

"So...you and Kevin are truly done?" Mom sat at the kitchen table and ran a hand through her hair, making it worse.

I resisted, mightily, the urge to go at least tamp it down with water, instead distracting myself by going to the cabinet for the kitty kibble. "We are done." My heart hurt, as it always did when I thought of Kevin. I took a breath. "And that's okay. Despite all the excitement, I've also already done a lot of thinking out here. I'm getting over Kevin and finding myself. I'm working on a stage play. I'm really making progress with it, Mom."

She nodded. "That's really nice. You think you won't ever go back to hair?"

"I don't know. I like doing hair too." I felt a little dismissed, though I suppose she just didn't know what to say. Mom was incredibly creative in her own way, especially in the garden, but all she ever wrote was emails and lists. The oven beeped, announcing that it had gotten to temperature; I put the bagels in and set a timer. "Most writers have a day job, you know." I thought about all my friends here on Orcas. "Or several day jobs, even."

Dad came down the hall, his hair still damp from the shower.

"I smell coffee! And are those our bagels?"

"You bet!" I went over and gave him a kiss. "Sleep well?"

"Perfectly!"

Thirty minutes later, we were seated cozily around my kitchen table, surrounded by crumbs, open cream cheese schmear containers, and our second cups of coffee. We had a daunting day of cooking and eating ahead of us, but right now, I felt confident we were up to the challenge.

"So!" Dad said, getting up and gathering the plates. "Who's on first?"

There was a knock on the front door. I jumped, and then laughed at myself. "I'll get it," I said, and headed out to the living room, James twining between my legs, trying to get me to trip over him, because that would just end so well for both of us.

"Good morning, Ms. Tate," said Kip, looking all sober and crisp in his uniform.

James darted between my feet and then Kip's on his way to who-knew-where.

"Ms. Tate?" I asked. "Official business, then?"

Kip smiled. "Afraid so. I've just got a few more questions. Mind if I come in?"

"Oh! Sure." I stepped back to let him in.

Mom and Dad had followed me to the living room. "Is this your friend? Will he be cooking in uniform?" Mom asked, her eyes widening as she took him in. On his belt, the radio gave a quiet crackle.

"No, he's..." I started. "I mean, yes, he's my friend too, but... not the one who's coming to dinner."

"Ah. Okay." Mom's eyes were still wide. And...appreciative?

Dad put his hand out. "Adam Jonas, and this is my wife, Lauren."

Kip shook Dad's hand. "Deputy Rankin. Pleased to meet you both. I just need a few minutes with your daughter here, if you don't mind?"

"I thought everything was all resolved about the…intrigue?" Mom asked.

"Resolved enough," Kip said. "This is about yesterday's incident."

"Yesterday's?" Mom looked at me.

I squirmed under her gaze before turning back to Kip. "I, um, well they got in late last night, there wasn't much chance to, you know, tell them much. Or, anything, really."

"I see." Kip glanced at my parents. "This should only take a few minutes. Then I'm sure Camille will be happy to fill you in."

"Okay, well, sure," Mom said. "We were just—the turkey…"

"Yeah. Right." Dad took her arm and they headed back to the kitchen. Mom looked over her shoulder at me quizzically as they went.

Kip led me to the armchair, and took a seat on the sofa beside it. "It's actually all right to tell your parents what's going on," he said gently. "Police business is in the public record."

And the whole island already knows every last detail, I thought. "I know." I shifted in the chair. "I just—it hadn't come up. I was going to tell them. I wanted to have a little normal Thanksgiving time first. Besides, it's true; they did get here late last night. They missed their second ferry. And we were just now finishing breakfast."

"Ah." He nodded. "Well, they seem like very nice parents."

"They are."

After a little awkward pause, Kip brought out his notebook and cleared his throat. "I wanted to clear up something about the timeline."

"Okay."

"You and Mr. Joseph Brixton were over here together at around three-thirty, correct?"

"Yes."

"No one else was here? Before Ms. Lisa Cannon arrived, is that right?"

"Yes. Just the two of us. And James. My cat?"

He glanced up, frowning. "I meant people, Cam."

"Right."

"And then Ms. Lisa Cannon came over, and the three of you immediately went to her house."

"Yes, pretty much. I mean, she told us there was an intruder, and we talked about what to do, but—yeah, we went over there."

"Okay. And how long did it take you to walk to her house?"

"Just a minute or two. There's a path."

"A path?"

"Between the estates. You've seen it; where the…where the last dead body was. The one that supposedly wasn't dead. I mean the murder that wasn't. And then was." My face was starting to flame up. "You know. My first day here." *The day we met.*

"Yes. Got it." He made some notes. "So it was not yet four o'clock when you entered Ms. Lisa Cannon's house."

"I guess so. I wasn't exactly looking at my watch, but that sounds right."

Kip leaned forward, searching my face as he asked, "And then the three of you entered the house, and discovered the body?"

"Not exactly." I shifted. "We immediately saw that the place was a mess, but then, well, Lisa sent me away."

"She did."

"And so I left, but then I hadn't barely gotten back to the path when I heard her scream and I went back to see if everything was all right."

Kip wrote something down without losing eye contact with me. "So you left the house, and then went back."

"Yes." I'd told him all this yesterday. Cops really did like their repetition, didn't they?

"Approximately how much time elapsed between when you left and when you returned? As close as you can judge it, Ms. Tate, I know you didn't look at your watch."

I felt my eyes widen, and my skin started to tingle, just the tiniest bit. "Just a minute or so…Kip, you don't think they…Lisa?"

He shook his head before looking down to write a more extensive note. "I don't think anything. I'm just trying to establish the exact timeline, as closely as possible."

"Okay." I struggled to remember exactly. "JoJo and Lisa said they could handle it—like, they really wanted to handle it. I think she was worried about stuff missing, and maybe I'd be in the way. So I left, and walked off her porch and down the stairs and across the lawn and to the path. Then I heard her scream, and I went back."

"Did you hurry back?"

"No…I, um, sort of didn't rush. The scream startled me." *I waited till I was done vanishing, anyway.* "I listened to hear if there was going to be another scream, but there wasn't. I was kind of scared, too, and I didn't know what was going on, or what I should do. But then I walked back, and knocked. JoJo let me in. And then…"

"Right." He made another short note. "So you didn't—"

We were interrupted by a knock at the door. "Oh!" I jumped up. "That'll be Colin."

Kip snapped his notebook shut and stood up as well. "All right, Camille, I think I've got all I need."

"You do?" I froze midway across the room. "Really?"

"For now." He smiled. "You might want to let your guest in before he feels the need to knock again."

"Right." I continued to the door, opening it to reveal a smiling Colin, bearing a cardboard carrier with four covered coffee cups. A string bag of potatoes was over one shoulder, and a pink box was wedged under the other arm. "Oh!"

"Just making a breakfast delivery," he said, stepping in. "Oh, hey, Deputy."

"I was just leaving," Kip said, nodding to us both. "I'll let you know if I need more information, Ms. Tate. You both have a nice Thanksgiving dinner, now."

"Thank you," I said. "You too…?"

Kip smiled. "I get off at noon. In theory, anyway." He shrugged. "Assuming we don't find any more bodies lying around."

"Right," Colin said. "Good luck with that."

I showed Kip to the door, though it wasn't hard to find. "Keep me posted," I ventured.

"Sure thing."

After he drove off, I turned to Colin. "So. Want to meet my parents?"

Colin grinned. "You bet."

೮೨

At last, something was going well. Mom and Dad both just *loved* Colin; I was already bracing myself for being pulled aside and browbeaten into admitting that I might actually consider dating him. He even provided enough of a distraction that they neglected to ask me why a cop had come by to question me, or what "yesterday's incident" might have been.

Colin deftly handled the enormous turkey, and we got it into the oven—unstuffed, as it happened; he said it would be juicier and would cook faster that way—before ten o'clock. Then he had Dad peeling potatoes and Mom working on making the stuffing—well, dressing, technically—which would cook most of the way on the top of the stove, only going into the oven to brown after the bird came out.

"Make your four o'clock dinner, no problem," Colin said, pausing to check Mom's work with the seasonings. "Who's hungry now?"

I started to say I was still full of bagels, but then Colin opened that pink box, revealing the most gorgeous, crazily decorated donuts I'd ever seen. They were all different—yellow and green and speckled with multicolored candy dots; deep dark chocolate; gleaming maple-colored with flecks of bacon—and then the aroma filled the air.

"I'm starving," I said, reaching for the darkest chocolate one.

"Well, I suppose..." Mom said, already biting into the maple-bacon.

A purple-sheened one near the back of the box caught Dad's eye. "That's not blueberry, is it?"

"Blueberry-sage-whiskey," Colin said, still smiling. "House specialty."

"Oh my god," I barely managed, around a luscious mouthful. "I didn't know there was a donut place on the island?"

"And open on Thanksgiving morning?" Mom added.

Colin chewed on a fritter-shaped delicacy. "Isn't," he said, after swallowing. "These came in special from Portland, flown in this morning. Got a source."

"Holy cats," I said, staring at him. "Seriously?" Oh, this was bad news. Very, very bad news indeed. I must never see this man again so long as I lived. I must kick him out of my house right this very moment. I must burn every memory of him from my brain.

He shrugged, the grin lighting an evil glint in his eye. "Just lucky I decided to share. This time."

I took another huge bite, savoring the rich chocolate, licking excess off my lips. Was everything here just tremendously, exquisitely delicious? Even foodie Kevin would find nothing to criticize in these artisanal donuts. "Well, given that I'm going to let you eat some of my succulent Thanksgiving turkey..."

"That I 'helped' you cook," he added, laughing. "All right! What's next, gang?"

"Oh! The stuffing," Mom said, dashing back to the stove.

Colin followed her. "It's great, nothing to worry about. Just needs a little stir."

"Got the potatoes on deck here," Dad said. "Whenever you're ready for them."

I smiled at him, trying not to let the sudden sadness that washed over me show. My brother Cliff loved, loved, loved mashed potatoes. So much that Mom always had to make double the amount, and then made him mash them himself, in penance for eating so many of them.

Why did my brother have to be so far away? Why did the world have to be so big?

∾

Smells of roasting turkey had now replaced the somewhat sickly-sweet aroma of donuts. I'd only had two…well, two and a half…and I never wanted to see them again.

The meat, however: that, I was looking forward to.

The aroma had apparently lured James back into the house from wherever he'd darted off to when Kip arrived. James lurked around the kitchen, nose and tail twitching, pretending he was just hanging out.

"Go ahead, try and open that oven door," I said to him. "I won't even stop you."

He gave me a fuzzy-faced glance before returning his gaze to the stove. He was actually splitting his attention between the oven and the stovetop, where a pan of giblets simmered. Colin and Mom both agreed those miserable-looking organ meat things belonged in the gravy. *Not if I have anything to do with it*, I told myself, but smiled and nodded at them. It's important not to antagonize confused people if you can help it.

"He wants the liver," Mom said.

He's as mad as the rest of you, I thought. Then again, look at what he ate normally. I'd have to be pretty desperate to consider his kibble edible.

My phone rang just as there was a knock on the front door. "Camille!" I heard Diana Brixton's voice ring out, even through the whole house. I pulled out my phone as I rushed up the hallway. Yes: she was calling my phone as well as pounding on my door and hollering. "Coming!" I yelled into the phone, even as my skin tingled with startlement.

I pushed through it. Nothing scary here. Just my boss. I pulled open the front door and there was Diana, actually literally wringing her hands. I didn't even see her phone. "Camille!" she cried, flowing into the house and plopping into one of the easy chairs. "Oh, thank goodness you're here!"

"What is it, Mrs. Brixton?" I followed her over and sat in the other chair. "I did stop by, did Clary tell you?"

"Who? Oh, Clary, of course. Yes."

Your own daughter? I thought, still smiling at my overwrought boss lady. Her sleek highlighted hair, usually so perfectly in order, already showed signs of needing a touch-up: strands protruded at the nape of her neck, and I could see the stripe of gray at her part. Wasn't she seeing Jennifer, like we'd agreed? My former salon-mate had access to all my client files and a deft hand with both base color and highlights. "What is the matter?" I prompted again.

"Oh! I don't know what could have happened, but I swear, somebody has been in the house."

I was chilled. "What? Is something missing?"

She shook her head, taking a deep breath. "Mark from Homemade is here to prepare our dinner, and he reports that the kitchen is not at all as he remembers. A roasting pan cannot be located, and the refrigerator temperature has been adjusted. And no one can find the salt!"

I gaped at her. "Um...well, I did stay there two nights when I moved here, but..." Had I roasted or chilled anything? Had I misplaced the salt? I didn't think so; I didn't have any food when I'd arrived. It was only a few short weeks ago. But so much had happened since then. "Do you—"

My front door opened and Clary burst in, at the same moment as Dad appeared from the hallway, coming to check out the commotion. "Mom," Clary said, "we found the roasting pan. And like ten gallons of salt. Come home." Then she noticed me, and then my dad. "Oh, hi."

"Um, hi?" *Great, Cam. Way to defend your home against invasion from snotty heiresses.* I got to my feet and gave Diana a hand up before introducing her, and Clary, to my dad. Mom showed up just in time to have to do it all over again. I just hoped Colin would stay put. And James.

I bundled the Brixton invasion out, following them to the front porch, and shut the door behind us. "I'm sorry, but I need to talk to you." Clary smirked, Diana looked irked. Having found her salt and her pan, she surely thought she was done with me. "Did JoJo tell you that there was a break-in at Lisa's yesterday?"

For once, Clary stopped smirking.

Diana's eyes bulged with alarm. She sputtered, "A break-in? At Lisa's?" I braced myself for the coming interrogation, but she turned and strode sternly back to her own house, Clary in tow.

JoJo had some explaining to do.

Well, I had discharged my duties as a caretaker. I'd let my boss know about a neighborhood threat in a timely manner. Maybe I wouldn't get fired, even though the salt had briefly been missing. Not to mention that errant roasting pan. I watched Diana's march back to the big house, and my cell phone rang again. I hadn't even realized I'd hung it up. I pulled it out: it was Jen.

"Hey," I said into the receiver, following my folks back to the kitchen. "What's up?"

"I heard Kip stopped out there again."

"Do you just have a police scanner in your van, or what?"

She laughed. "When are you going to stop wondering about how news travels on a tiny island?"

"When somebody finally shows me how it actually works. I'm a city girl, you know." At the stove, Colin gave me an inquisitive glance. The kitchen was feeling a bit crowded; I headed for the back door, nearly stepping on James in the process.

"Well? So what's the scoop?" Jen asked.

"I don't know. He just had more questions—or, well, mostly the same questions as before. About the timeline. When are *you* going to learn that I am not the county sheriff, and the cops don't report to me?"

"Oh, come on, Cam; you know he'd tell you stuff if you just asked him nice enough."

"I totally ask him stuff!" I protested. "He's all, *official police business*, blah blah blah."

She sighed theatrically. "I can see I've got my work cut out with you. Well, I gotta run—let me know if you hear anything!"

"You know I will."

I hung up the phone and went back inside. "Just a nosypants," I told everyone.

"Oh? What did Jen want to know?" Colin asked.

"Everything," I said.

Dad stood over the stove, stirring the potatoes. Mom had moved to the table where she was chopping Swiss chard. "Honey, do you—" she started, just as we heard a knock on the door.

Jeez. Was Diana Brixton going to run over here all day now? Stifling a sigh, I said, "Hang on, Mom," as I headed to the front door.

I composed my face into a polite smile and opened the door.

Then I stood there, gaping, as my brain froze.

I just could not make sense of it…it couldn't be…

"Cliff!" I finally shrieked, as my brother dropped his duffel bag and grabbed me into his arms for an engulfing hug. "Cliff, oh my god what are you *doing* here?!"

"It's Thanksgiving, isn't it?" he said into my hair, squeezing me tight enough to hurt my arm. I didn't even care. "Big family dinner thing? Mashed potatoes? Surely you've heard of it, Mealy?"

I was even happy to hear that awful nickname. I squeezed him back even harder. "You're in Thailand, you dork!"

He laughed, finally releasing me. "Apparently not! Thailand is much warmer than this."

I pulled back a little and looked him over, unable to stop grinning. "Do you not even own a sweater? Long pants? *Shoes?*"

"All in there." He pointed to the duffel at his feet. "I came straight from the airport, though; didn't want to miss the twelve-forty ferry."

"You sneak!"

By now, Mom and Dad had come to the door; Colin hung back behind them, a bemused grin on his face. "Clifford!" Mom cried, standing frozen in the middle of the room. She was clearly as surprised as I was.

So that could only mean…

I looked at Dad, who was unable to suppress a massive grin. "Pulled a hidden ball trick on your mom," he told me. "And you."

"Clifford!" Mom kept saying, even as she found her mobility again and began trying to elbow me out of the way. In a loving, motherly sort of way, of course. "Clifford!"

Colin cleared his throat politely.

"Oh! This is my brother, Cliff," I said, pointing to the combined person that was my mother smothering Cliff in a hug. "And Cliff, this is my, er, friend, Colin."

Cliff grinned over the top of Mom's head. "You've been here, what, three weeks and you already have an Er, Friend?"

My face flamed with embarrassment. What? I wasn't interested in Colin. If I were going to be not-interested in anyone on this crazy island, it would be Kip. Who I was not interested in. Not interested! Despite his lush curls and golden voice.

And not JoJo either. Who didn't live here. Which was a good thing.

"Pleased to meet you, Cliff," Colin said, putting out a hand, giving my brother a plausible excuse for disentangling himself from Mom's embrace.

"And you, Colin the Friend."

My eyes widened as I looked at my friend, but he just laughed. Cliff could disarm anyone—he was so relaxed and good-natured, he just put folks at ease. It let him get away with murder, let me tell you. I mean, not *literally*, of course. But I liked him a lot better now that we weren't kids together.

"Well, come on in," Dad said, reaching for Mom's hand. She still seemed at a loss for any words beyond my brother's name. "Don't know where you're gonna sleep in this little house, but I guess we'll figure something out."

"Sleep!" I said, my brain scrambling. "Yeah, um, I've only got one guest bedroom here…"

"Couch!" Cliff said, walking over and dropping his duffel bag on it. "This looks perfectly comfy. Just scrounge up some blankets and I'll be great."

I started to head for the hallway to check the guest closet when the sound of a loud, struggling motor came through the open front door. James darted in, obviously terrified by whatever was making that racket, an orange blur flashing past all the people on his way to the kitchen. I hadn't even seen him go out again.

I walked back to see what in the world was coming around the Brixtons' house. Because clearly it wasn't stopping there.

The biggest RV I'd ever seen came laboring around the curved drive. It slowed as it reached the guesthouse, looking unsure how to maneuver around all the other vehicles already parked here—my Honda, Mom & Dad's Lexus, Colin's red pickup, and a small white rental car that was clearly Cliff's. The RV faltered, slowing further before just coming to a stop in the middle of what remained of the open space, blocking everyone in. INTRUDER was emblazoned across its front.

"Well, that's certainly straight out of left field," Dad remarked. "Were you expecting someone else?"

"No," I said, heading for the door. "It's probably someone for the Brixtons, maybe they got lost. I'll let them know—"

I had barely stepped onto the front porch when the Intruder's driver door opened.

And my ex-boyfriend, Kevin, climbed out.

CHAPTER 5

My heart stopped.

Oh, Kevin was just as I'd left him. Long legs, narrow hips, sweet full lips, high cheekbones crowned with almond-shaped eyes that glowed green against the tawny smoothness of his skin. His hair was still in dreadlocks and my heart was still in tatters. I just stood staring at him, my mouth hanging open. I'd have thought my capacity for surprise had been burned out by Cliff's arrival, but this… He gave me a shy and hopeful grin.

"Kevin?" I finally managed. Not the most intelligent thing to say, but it *was* his name.

"Cam." He walked across the gravel drive to me and reached for my hand.

I drew my hand away and took a step back. "Wait, what—no! You can't, you can't just come here and do this! Not *now*."

His smile grew. He was *confident*, the handsome bastard. "If not now, when?"

"No! Just…just turn that crazy thing around and get out of here. Where did you *get* that?"

"It's sort of a story, Cam. I can show you the inside if you like, and explain, and talk."

Did he *seriously* think I was going to *tour* that…that…*Intruder*? With *him*? Just because he was brash enough to show up in it? "You can't be here! Get that thing out of my driveway! Get it off this island!"

Kevin shrugged. "I can't. The next ferry doesn't leave for hours yet. And I don't have a reservation." He gave me a helpless grin and a sexy shrug. "I probably can't even get one. Space for vehicles like this is pretty limited. I was lucky to get here at all on a holiday weekend."

My parents had now followed me outside, and were alternately smiling at Kevin, ("Hi dear!" My mother cooed hopefully, while Kevin smiled back) and whispering to one another. I had no idea what Colin and Cliff were doing, and at this point, I just didn't care. Hopefully they were in the kitchen, mashing potatoes. Or whatever. Not being crazy. That would be good: somebody, somehow, somewhere in my day, not doing something crazy and unexpected and—

"Camille?"

Diana Brixton came around the main house.

"Oh, Mrs. Brixton—" I started.

She was staring at the Intruder, a look of naked horror on her face. "Camille Tate, what in the world is this? It was not on the application form." She tore her eyes away long enough to take in the rest of the cars. "In fact, only this Lexus was."

"Mom!" came Clary's voice, from a third-floor window in the main house. "Mom, JoJo won't give me the brandy back!"

Diana froze, caught between conflicting imperatives.

I dove into the breach. "Mrs. Brixton, I am terribly sorry. Kevin...stopped by and was just leaving." I gave my ex-boyfriend a fierce look. "You see?" I said to him. "You can't stay here. You can't park this thing here. And, by the way, in case you had somehow forgotten, we're not speaking to each other!"

His face fell, just a bit, and he took a step back toward the monstrosity. "But, Cam..."

So of course that's when I started to feel sorry for him. Looking all crestfallen like that, he had just the face I'd fallen in love with...years ago, when times were good. When I'd thought he was humble, and sweet, and caring. Not a pretentious hipster with a heart of artisanal, locally sourced and hand-hewn ice cubes.

I steeled my own heart. "Kevin Ndoye, if you had something to say to me, you could have phoned me. You could have sent an email. You could have dispatched a carrier pigeon. Instead, you drive up in this"—I waved at the stupid vehicle— "...*thing*—and come all this way, to interrupt a family gathering and probably screw up my new job! Oh!" I stomped my foot, hating myself for the childishness of the gesture, but it was either that or slug him. "This is just so like you."

"Cam?" Colin called from the doorway. "Everything all right out here?"

Kevin's eyes widened as he took in the hunky boat builder. He seemed to see the weather-beaten red pickup truck for the first time as well.

"Mom!" Clary shrieked from the main house.

"Don't listen to her!" came JoJo's voice, from an adjacent window. "It's for her own good! You said no drinking before we eat! Caviar doesn't count!"

"Children!" Diana Brixton shouted, loud enough to carry to her offspring.

In my pocket, my cell phone rang. "Because of course," I muttered, reaching in to click the ringer off without even looking at it.

Colin walked out and came to stand beside me in an obvious protector posture. The gesture both warmed my heart and infuriated me, so I kept my eyes on Kevin. "You heard my boss. Get back in this thing and drive it away from here."

Kevin took an uncertain step toward the Intruder.

Across the lawn, Clary shrieked again, leaning far out the window. JoJo laughed from the next window over, holding a half-full bottle of something amber-colored dangling over the ground three stories below. "Come and get it!" he taunted his sister.

We all stared at the big house. Diana found her footing the

soonest, turning to charge back over there. "Joseph Brixton, don't you dare drop that on the patio!"

She was interrupted by someone in the window behind JoJo. I caught a flash of dark hair and a triumphant female shriek, followed quickly by JoJo's cry of distress and betrayal as the someone wrestled the bottle from him and vanished back into the house.

"Ha!" Clary cried from her window, before also vanishing.

The rest of us stood another long moment, still staring at the main house.

"Is it usually this exciting around here?" my mother finally ventured.

"No," I said. "Except when it is." In my pocket, my cell phone vibrated with a new incoming call.

That's when Cliff appeared at the front door of the guesthouse. "What's up? What did I miss? Oh—hi, Kevin. I didn't know you were invited." He darted a glance to me.

Kevin shifted on his feet. "Hey, Cliff, good to see you, man. It's uh, supposed to be a surprise." He smiled his winning smile and lifted his hands, palms up. "Surprise?"

My mother laughed.

I looked at my parents. I looked at the Intruder. I looked at my ex-boyfriend, and at my new er-friend, and at my beloved brother. James poked his head out the front door; I looked at my cat. A soft mist started to fall, and I began to shiver. The phone in my pocket vibrated again.

"All right," I said. "Everybody in the house. We'll work this out in there."

∽

Mom had been heating up cider on the stove, with Colin advising her on the spices. She now brought us all steaming mugs of amazingness as we crowded into the living room. I hadn't realized how small this room actually was until I tried to stuff six people and an inquisitive kitten in it.

"That's quite a story," my father said. I'd been filling them in on the details of the kidnapping and the intrigue of my first few weeks on Orcas, including how I'd witnessed a shooting and found Megan Duquesne's body, only to be locked up by a crazy woman. Two murders and my own kidnapping. I'd conveniently left out the fact that I'd been shot, of course. I knew that would send my parents into a protective tailspin that would end with my being bodily removed from the island, no matter what I had to say about it. "I'm glad it's all under control, sweetie."

"Yes. Me too." But my stitches hurt, and I was worried about Lisa's break-in, and I wished I could just tell them everything. But of course, I never told anyone everything, did I? I always had to leave out something, especially my own talent for chameleoning in the face of danger.

But talking about it, even the heavily edited version, was upsetting. I shivered.

"I'll light another fire," Cliff said. He'd been watching me silently while I talked. I always wondered how much he actually understood about what was different about me. He got to work balling up newspaper and setting out kindling. Within a couple of minutes, he had a healthy fire roaring. I guess living in the tropics hadn't squelched all his Pacific Northwest knowledge.

"Is that woman really going to make me park the RV somewhere else?" Kevin asked.

After the story I'd just told, I couldn't believe Kevin was worried about his stupid RV. "Of course she is," I snapped. "You heard her. She made my *parents* fill out an entire questionnaire before allowing them on the property."

My dad shrugged, sipping his cider. "Oh, it wasn't so bad. No worse than applying for a bank loan or a passport." He grinned.

I gave him a small smile before turning back to Kevin. "How did you find this place, anyway? I'm sure I never told you where I was." *I didn't tell you anything*, I thought. *I vanished.*

Kevin gave me a steady look. "Well…there've been some interesting news stories coming off Orcas Island in the last week or two. It wasn't too hard to put enough facts together. How many Camille Tates are there?" He shrugged. "I'm sorry, Cam. I didn't mean to piss you off. I should have…I mean, I wasn't really thinking it through. What I read scared me. I needed to get here and make sure you were okay."

Maybe that's why he wasn't acting surprised—he'd already heard about everything on the local news.

"Seems a little late to figure out that you care about somebody," Colin put in. He was standing by the crackling fire, looking tall and rugged and imposing. Surely unintentionally.

"Yeah, swing and a miss, I'd say," Dad put in.

Mom gave me her concerned, loving-mother face. "Can I get you more cider, Camille?"

"We could probably all use some," I said. "Spiked, preferably."

"I'll get it!" Cliff leapt up and bounded down the hall to the kitchen.

In my pocket, my phone buzzed again. Who in the world kept calling me? "Hang on," I said to everyone as I pulled it out. Oh jeez: Kip. He'd already called once before, and Jen had called twice as well. "I've got to take this." I got up and headed into the hallway after Cliff, looking for a quiet place to answer it.

And nearly bumped into my brother, who was hurrying back to the front room. "Hey, shouldn't the oven be on?"

"What?" I said, even as I was already swiping the call open. "Hold on, Kip, I've got an emergency here," I said into the phone, and then to Cliff, "What do you mean?"

"The oven's cold. You've got a big raw turkey in there."

"You are kidding me!"

Mom stepped into the hall behind us as Kip's tinny voice came out of the phone in my hand: "Ms. Tate? Are you there?"

"Yes!" I brought the phone back to my ear and turned away from the kitchen crisis, ducking into my bedroom and pulling the door shut behind me. "What is it?"

"You said there's an emergency? What—"

"No, I meant—no emergency."

He gave a relieved sigh. "So, everything's all right over there?"

"No!" I choked back a sudden lump in my throat. "No, Kip, it isn't. My brother showed up from *Thailand* and my ex-*boyfriend* showed up from Seattle, and Diana is pissed at me and, and, and, now my turkey isn't cooking and we're supposed to eat in less than two hours!"

"What? Why, um—" I could almost hear him scrambling to figure out what to respond to first.

I caught my breath and tried to calm down, sitting down on the bed and kicking off my shoes. "Oh Kip, I'm sorry. We'll figure it out. It's just—everything's happening at once."

"All right." He sounded dubious, if still relieved. "You're sure you don't need any help there? I'm able to come by, if needed."

"Can you magically make a turkey cook?" I laughed. "No, seriously. But that's why I couldn't answer earlier. I mean, all of it."

"Understood."

"So why are you calling? Is something wrong? I mean, somewhere other than here?"

He gave his mellifluous chuckle, then got serious. "No, not at all. I just wanted to let you know that we're downgrading the investigation into Snooks's death."

"Downgrading?"

"It's not murder. We think the old fellow died of a heart attack."

"Oh. That's good? I guess?"

He paused. "Yes. It is good. It means everyone's safe, and there's no larger conspiracy surrounding you, or Ms. Cannon, or anyone down there on Massacre Bay. Just a series of odd coincidences, a break-and-enter gone wrong."

"Really? You think it's all coincidence?"

Another very slight pause. "No, actually, I don't. What I do think is that all the press attention garnered by the most recent excitement around there attracted the notice of Mr. Snooks. He was notably unstable; it's why he was a loner in the first place. I think he got it in his head to go poke around the house belonging to a wealthy person who lived alone. This wasn't like Ephraim. I believe the stress of actually committing a burglary was so overwhelming that he had a heart attack." Kip gave a sympathetic exhale.

"But if this wasn't like him, why..."

"He was quite poor, Cam. He lived outside the system, and had no income. Winters are hard here. Desperation drives us to nefarious deeds at times."

"Yeah." I thought about Lisa's ransacked house. She'd be all day putting it back together. Maybe the actors could help. Or JoJo could. She seemed to trust him...I remembered her tight-lipped, worried face. "So, nothing's missing at Lisa's?"

Kip paused for longer this time. "Ms. Tate, I cannot comment on—"

"Really, Kip?" I interrupted him. "You just called to tell me there's no investigation!"

He sighed. "I called to tell you the investigation has been downgraded. That there was no murder. There was still a crime committed, and that's all I can tell you."

"Okay, fine. But Lisa doesn't really live alone. The actors are in and out of there all day and all night. And until recently, so was Sheila."

"Cam, Ephraim wouldn't know that."

"Everyone on this island seems to know everything."

Maybe I sounded a little snippy, because Kip's voice softened again. "Perhaps you're right. But I just wanted to let you know you could relax."

"I wish I could!" In the hall outside my bedroom door, I could hear Mom's and Cliff's voices, and then Dad joining them.

"What's the current situation with your turkey?" Kip asked.

"I don't know! I need to go deal with it."

"All right. Have a, well, a happy Thanksgiving?"

I gave a helpless laugh. "Thanks. Same to you." I clicked the phone off. It immediately lit up with a call: Jen. "Hey," I said into the phone, "can I call you back in a few minutes?"

"What's going on?!"

"Insanity! Seriously, I'll call you right back. I promise." I hung up before she could respond, took another deep breath, and got up off my bed.

In the kitchen, everyone was now crowded around the stove, which had been pulled out from the wall. Dad and Colin sat on the floor, peering at the back of the miserable appliance.

"Get those wires too," Colin said. Dad grunted and reached in, holding a soiled cloth. "Get around that whole area."

Kevin hovered over both of them. I could just see his chef-identity dying to burst forth, though he was trying hard to contain himself.

"What's wrong with it?" I asked.

"Dunno," Colin said. "Looks like it shut itself off when it got hot. Kinda the opposite of what an oven's supposed to do."

"It was working for a while," I said. "The turkey was starting to cook; we could all smell it. It went for like an hour, at least."

"Wires are all gunked up," Dad said, his voice partially muffled. "You don't use this thing much?"

"Well, no, Dad," I said, thinking about it. "I guess this was my first time. I just moved here, you know."

"I guess the previous tenant didn't do much baking either."

"Um." I thought about the previous tenant. Megan Duquesne… who washed up dead on the beach last week. For me to find. I shivered, rubbed my arms, shook my head to clear away the sad image. "I guess not."

"There!" Dad said, scooting back out from behind the stove. The whole back of his shirt was covered in dust and schmutz. "Try it now."

Colin turned the dial. We all leaned in. The light had come

on…the temperature gauge read 100 degrees, its starting position…it still read 100…we waited, breathless…then it clicked over to 101! "Yes!" I cried.

"Hooray!" Mom shouted.

"How much time did we lose?" I asked, peering through the dark glass window. "How will we know how much longer to cook it for? Is the turkey still safe to eat?"

Kevin stood a little taller. Ah yes, at last, his area of expertise. "You do have a poultry thermometer, right?"

"Um…" I started rummaging through kitchen drawers.

"Just tug on the drumsticks," Colin said. "They wiggle loose, you know you're done."

Kevin gave him a dark and disdainful look. "If you want the whole house to come down with salmonella, sure."

"Cut it out, you two," I said. "Kevin, if you're gonna stay for the meal, you can't keep insulting the other guests."

Kevin turned to look at me, his face soft and hopeful. "Does this mean you're letting me stay?"

I shrugged. "Where else are you going to go?"

"Awwwwww," my brother said, pulling us both into goofy sideways hugs. "You two are adorable."

From across the room, Colin gave me an unreadable look.

"So," Mom started, as the front door exploded in ferocious knocking.

"What now!" I cried, rushing to open it before whoever it was could beat a hole in it.

"Oh, thank god you're home," JoJo said, bursting past me and flopping down on my couch, resting his head on Cliff's duffel bag and throwing me an insouciant grin. "You will never *believe* the madness going on over there." There was that strange quasi-British accent again. He waved in the general direction of the main house with a three-quarters-empty brandy bottle, before holding the bottle up to me. "Drink?"

My phone rang. "Jen!" I cried into it after I swiped it open.

"You said you were going to call me right back! I'm about to drive out there and drop in on your dinner!"

"You might as well! You'd be the last person left on the island who hasn't," I said, walking toward the back of the house, leaving the rest of my family and assorted guests and interlopers to deal with JoJo. I went into my bedroom again and pulled the door shut behind me, flopping on the bed once more.

"Really? Who's there?"

"Oh Jen, you wouldn't believe it." I gave her a brief recap of the day so far. Even just the highlights took like ten minutes.

"Wow!" she said, giggling.

"It's not funny."

She gave one final snort. "I know, but it also kind of is."

Well, maybe she had a point there, but I wasn't going to concede it to her. "So what's up? Why aren't you at your thing? You're not calling from your thing, are you?"

"Oh! Jeez. It got canceled. Katrina came down with the flu this morning. So the rest of us have just been hanging out at the bar, eating pickles and olives. I thought I'd invite myself to your dinner—then I thought I was too late—but apparently not!"

I laughed. "Shoot, why not? I have the world's biggest turkey, and it won't be ready for hours. Come on down."

"Great! See you in a few."

I went back to the kitchen after I hung up. Dad was in there, adding the last of JoJo's brandy to a tray full of cups of hot cider. "We need to cook some more potatoes," I told him.

⁂

It was six o'clock. Thanksgiving dinner, which was supposed to have been served two hours ago, was finally coming along nicely. By that I mean the turkey was turning golden-brown and smelling delicious again, though Kevin and Colin both (begrudgingly) agreed that it needed at least another hour in the oven. Potatoes—including the extra batch—had been mashed, and now sat on the back of the stove keeping warm. The stuffing was ready, similarly waiting. My crazy party had made its way through the brandy-spiked ciders, four bottles of wine, and I don't even know how many beers.

Only the fact that Mom had brought out a plate of crackers and cheese a while back had saved us from utter drunken debauchery.

Now Jen was in the front room, entertaining everyone with tales of bartending. I'd snuck off to the kitchen, ostensibly to check on things and feed James (the roasting-turkey smell was making him even crazier than the rest of us), but really just to catch a breather. Going from living alone on this vast estate, to all the intrigue of the last few weeks, to today's chaos: it was all a bit much.

I heard footsteps in the hallway and rearranged my face to "social" mode, relaxing when I saw that it was just my brother Cliff. He wandered in and gave me a smile. "Hey sis," he said, sipping a cold beer and then setting it on the kitchen table. "Is everything okay?"

I blushed and buried my nose in my wine for a moment. "You mean, after I sent you that long crazy email?"

"Well, you have to admit, it was quite a story."

I gazed at him. "You didn't come all the way across the ocean just to eat turkey and hug your family. Or even for mashed potatoes. You came because of that email."

He shrugged, not denying it. "Skype is all well and good, but sometimes, it just doesn't cut it. Sometimes you have to see for yourself." He peered at me. "You look good, at least."

"Well, thanks!" I laughed. "So do you."

He glanced down at his trim, tanned self. "The tropics, man. You gotta love 'em."

"Do you actually get any work done there?" Cliff was on a renewable six-month contract working for an international consulting firm. It had been renewed five times already. "You're never actually coming back to live in the States again, are you?"

"Can you blame me?" He laughed, sipping his beer. "Yeah, probably in another year or so. After much longer than that, I hear expats have a hard time readjusting."

"I believe it." I pulled up a chair at the table and sat down; he sat across from me. "Cliff, though I'm sorry I scared you enough to spend the money to get all the way over here, I'm so glad you're here. I miss you."

He reached over and tousled my hair. "I miss you too. I miss the folks, of course; but we're partners in crime, kid. You know?"

Cliff was only a little bit older than me; he'd been going on five when Mom and Dad had taken me in at the age of four. Sure, we'd had our moments, but overall, he'd been the best brother anyone could ever have wanted in the whole wide world. He protected and defended me, sharing his parents and home and life without a murmur. Sometimes growing up, when I saw other sibling relationships, I wondered if he was some kind of bodhi-sattva or something. I was a shy, frightened, closed-off little girl, and I was only supposed to be part of their family temporarily. But somehow, Cliff had found the patience and generosity to share his family with me for over twenty years. Not without some teasing, some mischief, of course. But I suppose his pranks and mischief lightened me up a little, got me laughing and showed me a few ways to deal with fear besides vanishing.

I was proud of him, and pleased that he was doing exactly what he wanted in life, and in paradise to boot; but I also just plain hated that he was so far away.

I sipped my wine again and grinned at my brother. "Partners in crime indeed. With you gone, I had to recruit Jen to solve mysteries with me."

He glanced down at the table with a small smile. "She's...en-ergetic."

A sudden whoop of laughter from the front room punctuated this statement. Yes, Jen Darling was every bit the ebullient redhead. "She's great," I said. "It's not always easy for me to make friends." My brother snorted at this understatement as I went on, "But she befriended me, well, the right way. She's really fun and nice and outgoing, but I also don't feel like she…" I paused, trying to figure out how to put it.

"She's not an emotional vampire?" Cliff said.

"Exactly. I feel like she likes me, that she wants to get to know me, but that she doesn't *need* me. You know?" He nodded. "Which is fine, since we both know I have trouble with letting my guard down."

"I like her," my brother said. "She seems like good people."

We sat quietly another minute or so, listening to the friendly chaos in the other room. Shy women, like me, tend to attract a certain kind of person—both romantically and friend-wise. Outgoing, confident-seeming people, yet ones in search of an audience. For acclaim, for validation?

Lisa Cannon might be one of those strong, confident women. I'd already wondered if my friendship with her—if that's what it was—was destined to go the direction of what I'd experienced with other strong girls and women I'd known from childhood onward.

Yet the memory of her panicked, frightened face yesterday in my kitchen…was it cruel of me to cherish that, just a tiny bit? I didn't want Lisa to be miserable. But it was a relief to know she was human.

Jen, however, just seemed uncomplicatedly outgoing. And she was doing a great job entertaining *my* family and guests. I hauled myself to my feet. "We should get back out there."

"Yep," Cliff said. "I was actually sent back to fetch you, but I didn't know if I'd get another chance to talk to you alone." He got up too and pulled me into a gentle hug, then released me. "It's good to see you, sis."

"You too, bro."

ഗ

At last, dinner was served. My table, which had initially been set for four, was stretched beyond its limit to accommodate the eight people who now sat around it. Though the Brixtons (or, rather, their hired chef) had served their own dinner at two, JoJo agreed to join us for a second feast. I hadn't invited him, exactly; somehow, he and my dad, of all people, had hit it off famously. They kept talking sports. Of all things.

We'd pulled the table out from its usual position against the window, and still we all barely fit into the kitchen. The turkey, in all its half-carved glory, sat on the counter; James sat on the floor just below it, tail flicking alertly.

"I'm watching you, Cat," I called out.

Flick.

"Pass the potatoes?" Jen asked. "And the gravy? This gravy is amazing, Mrs. Tate," she added, licking her fork.

"Seconds already?" Mom exclaimed. "I haven't even started eating my firsts yet!"

Cliff and I both busted out laughing. Mom did that every holiday: organizing the serving, and dishing up her own plate, with such care and attention that her food was almost cold by the time she actually took a bite.

"I have to admit," JoJo said, around a mouthful of turkey, "when I saw this monster on the counter yesterday, I didn't have high hopes for it."

"Not to mention the oven dying in the middle of roasting!" Cliff put in.

Kevin, across the table from me, sat a little taller. "Well, there is a method for cooking large poultry that calls for an hour of high roasting, then a rest, before finishing at a baking temperature. Of course, it needs to be done according to the right specifications to avoid salmonella. But the results are delicious."

I fought the urge to roll my eyes, instead just looking around the table. Nobody else seemed to find him insufferable: Cliff and my folks nodded at his words. Jen was listening to him politely, though perhaps did I see a tiny smile at the corner of her mouth?

I looked back at him, flicking a lock out of his face, warming to his audience. I'd been so miserable when we'd broken up. I'd been desperate, heartbroken, thinking no one would ever love me. That I'd missed my only chance. That had been only a month ago. And yet, in that time…well, quite a bit had changed.

I glanced over at Colin, sitting next to me. He had been addressing all his attention to his full plate, which had quickly become an empty plate. "More?" I asked him.

He looked up and smiled at me as he put a hand on his completely flat belly. (No, I was not looking at his physique at the Thanksgiving table!) "Need to take a minute to ponder first," he said.

"I'll take more," JoJo said, pushing his plate forward.

"More what?" Mom said, leaping to her feet.

"Mom!" I said. "Sit down and eat! JoJo can get his own seconds."

"Thirds," he said, but he did sidle to his feet and wander over to the turkey with his plate. James refused to relinquish his position on the floor. "Is it all right if I step on this cat?" JoJo asked.

"Be my guest," I said. "Maybe it'll teach him a lesson."

James darted out of the way just in time.

JoJo piled some slices of meat on his plate and set a drumstick on top of it.

"Where do you put all that?" Jen asked him.

JoJo grinned as he returned to the table. "If you're real nice to me, I'll show you later."

Jen rolled her eyes. "I've been rejecting you for over a decade." She grinned at my brother, bringing him in to her joke. "I swear, I thought I was done with bad pickup lines when I left the bar."

My dad guffawed. "Strike two!"

JoJo laughed good-naturedly before tucking into his thirds.

My own belly was getting full. Isn't it just the height of un-fairness, to spend all day preparing an absolute feast, of all your favorite things, only to find yourself stuffed before you've hardly started enjoying it? I paused to take a few deep breaths, trying to tamp the food down and make more room. The conversation around me flowed comfortably. Everyone was laughing and teas-ing and eating. My parents were here. My *brother* was here, in person! Sure, my ex-boyfriend was also here; but he was more or less behaving himself. And he'd be gone soon, so I could get back to my new life.

Maybe it wasn't the Thanksgiving I'd had in mind. It was much, much better.

CHAPTER 6

Cleanup was easy, if a little chaotic, with so many people helping. At a certain point, I quietly stepped out onto the back porch. Nobody noticed I'd left, which was fine with me.

A flash of orange caught my eye at the edge of the lawn. "James?" I called.

I heard a distant *meow* as he darted further away.

"Oh no you don't," I said, starting across the lawn. "You've been outside enough today. Did you steal some bones or something? Get back here!"

Not even a flick of a tail this time. Who had spoiled this cat so badly?

Oh, right: that would be me.

I stopped in the middle of the back lawn and looked up at the sky. It hadn't rained all day, though it had been cloudy; now, stars were out. It was remarkably peaceful. It never got old, how quiet and calming Orcas Island was.

Well, most of the time. When I wasn't being kidnapped or threatened, and my neighbor wasn't being broken into by a crazy boat dude who trashed her house and then died on her living room floor the day before Thanksgiving.

I wondered how Lisa was doing. Had she gotten her place cleaned up at least? Was she cooking for the actors, or had she gone out? I hoped she wasn't there all alone.

I walked around to the front of the guesthouse, cringing again at the sight of the massive Intruder parked behind all our cars, and then around the main house, trying to peer through the trees to Lisa's house. I couldn't hear anything, but then again, it was a little too far for that. But I ought to be able to see lights, I thought.

The main Brixton house was ablaze with lights, making it hard to see next door. I walked across the front drive toward the path that separated the two estates. James had come this way, I thought; I told myself I was just looking for my stupid cat.

It was even partly true.

In a minute, I had crossed over to Lisa Cannon's estate. I could see one light burning in a kitchen window, but since most of her windows faced the water, the place might be full of merry-making people and I'd just never know.

But I should have heard something by now, if so. Was she all alone here?

Before I could talk myself out of it, I walked up her front steps and knocked.

As I stood there waiting, it occurred to me that, nervous as it made me to be this unaccustomedly forward, my skin wasn't tingling at all. I was in no danger of chameleoning away. I liked Lisa, and I trusted her, I told myself.

Well, that and the fact that I'd been drinking all day. Alcohol really calmed down my chameleoning tendencies.

The door opened. Lisa stood there, a look of surprise briefly crossing her face before she gave me a relieved smile. "Oh, Cam. What's up?"

I shrugged, smiling back at her. "I just…my house is super full of people, and I was worried about you. How are you doing?"

She took a step back from the door into the entryway. "Come on in. Do you want a glass of wine?"

I followed her, laughing. "No thanks. I think I've had a case already. I just wanted to see how you were. After…you know."

"I know." She gave her tinkling laugh as she led me down the few steps into the immaculate living room. "All cleaned up, as you can see."

"That must have been a lot of work."

"The actors helped me. And JoJo."

"Really? He's at my place now; he's been there all afternoon. Do you think he's spending any time at all with his own family?"

Lisa sat on the sofa and motioned for me to sit next to her. I did. "Not if he can help it, I'm sure," she said. "Apparently, even his beloved sister has turned against him."

"Beloved sister?" I thought of the cool, sleek creature I'd met at the Brixtons' front door yesterday, her smirking drop-by with her mother, her shrieking out the window across the yard at him this morning. "What's she done?"

Lisa gave me a wry smile. "Brought a girlfriend, I hear."

"I...oh. Oh!" I shook my head. "Have you spoken with Diana and Emmett? I mean, are they, did they—" Now I could feel my face flushing, though thankfully, the rest of my skin remained calm. "I told Diana about the break-in this morning, and she didn't take it that badly, all things considered."

"I'm sure she was just building up steam. Apparently she was quite angry that JoJo hadn't told her. He was rather dramatic about it all; I'm not quite sure what happened over there. Truthfully, he should join my troupe. He has such a flair about him."

"That he does," I agreed, wondering why he hadn't mentioned any of this at my house. I glanced down at the coffee table, now wishing I had a glass of wine after all, just to have something to do with my hands. The table was perfectly tidy, just like the rest of the room. "So, did you do anything for Thanksgiving, or have you just been alone here all day? I mean, after the cleanup?" I added, stupidly realizing she'd just told me about everyone being here helping her.

"Oh, the holiday isn't a big deal to me," she said. "My ex-husband's family all had to get together at a great-aunt's house every year. Something like forty-five people came, and it was quite the production. I wasn't sure anybody other than the smallest children ever actually enjoyed it. Since the divorce, I find it nice to spend holidays on my own."

"Okay. But still, Lisa." I thought about it a minute. "I mean, you could come over to my place for dessert if you wanted. We have three kinds of pie."

She shook her head. "Thank you, but I think I just want to stay in and do nothing that involves putting on shoes." She looked at me with some surprise. "But you haven't had dessert yet? Did you eat late?"

I laughed. "Very late. Not that we meant to." I told her the whole story of the day.

"Oh, Cam!" she exclaimed, giving me that look of gentle chiding disappointment that she must have perfected working in the tech industry. "My oven works perfectly. You didn't have to have everyone on the floor doing a repair job."

I shrugged. "Well, I need an oven, don't I? And now it works."

"If you say so."

"I'm just glad all those helpful men were there to do the job," I said, just to see if I could get her to give that look again.

She was smarter than that, though, and merely laughed. "Of course."

I suddenly realized I'd been over here a while, without having told anyone where I was going, or even that I was going anywhere. I got to my feet. "Well, I should head on home. Thanks for the sanity break."

She got up as well and walked me to the front door. "Any time. I value your company, Cam. You know that."

"I'm just glad you're all right. That must have been so scary, to have all your stuff gone through like that. Even before you found the…the man who…dropped dead in here."

A shadow passed across her face briefly. "Yes, it was terrifying. I'm probably not completely over it yet; I'm just trying not to think too hard about it."

"And I'm happy that nothing's missing." I opened the front door and stepped out. Was I fishing? Sure, I was fishing.

Lisa stood in the doorway, looking like she wanted to say something more. Then she said, "Have a nice dessert. Say hello to your family for me."

"I will."

I started to head across the driveway and lawn toward the path through the trees, but stopped halfway. It was awfully dark in there. Sure, I'd walked over here in the dark; yet somehow now it seemed darker.

My first morning here came rushing back to me. When I'd watched Sheila shoot down a man in cold blood. Gregory Baines, once-famous commercial fisherman (well, according to Jen; he'd appeared on some sort of reality TV show for a couple of seasons). A man without anyone in the world, it seemed; no one to notice he was missing, to wonder if he were all right. No one even knew he was dead, until I told Kip everything that Sheila had revealed to me during her kidnapping of me, and insisted that the sheriff's deputy look into it.

By now, I had thoroughly spooked myself. I did not want to walk down that dark path.

I turned and walked up Lisa's driveway toward the road, only to again stop myself. There was another option, and it might even be safer than a no-shoulder, winding country road at night. Turning once more, I crossed her lawn and found the steep path that led to Lisa Cannon's dock.

It was so steep, it was actually a neat wooden staircase at times. I climbed down, not worried that she would see me. I'd been down on her rocky beach a couple of times, with Jen; you couldn't see Lisa's house from below. So it would stand to reason that you couldn't see the dock from the house, even if Lisa were watching for it.

When I emerged on the shingle, I took a moment to gaze out at the water. Still my favorite part of living on the island, even if these were the waters of Massacre Bay. There was no moon tonight, but the starlight made tiny ribbon-like designs on the gently stirring water. Gorgeous.

I started walking again, only to pause once more and look at her dock. Gregory Baines's boat was gone, and another boat was tied up. Of course: Gregory's poky, nameless little fiberglass craft must have been the boat that Sheila took when she fled. She'd been tracked to Crane Island, Kip had told me, and had left behind blood and a suicide note. But no body—or boat—had been found.

Crane Island. That's where the late Ephraim Snooks had lived—no, he didn't live there, but he shuttled people there, apparently. Was it a coincidence? Did he have anything to do with Sheila?

Either way, this other boat had to be his. Despite my growing urgency to get back to my house full of guests, I walked over to Lisa's dock for a closer look.

It was a far more interesting boat than Gregory's, that was for sure. I could certainly believe that an eccentric old coot had lived on it. If a chicken shack had been built inside a large rowboat, roofed with rusty corrugated metal, then painted with leftover cans of paint from an elementary school remodel project, this might be the result. It must have started life as a fishing boat, but had been so tweaked and added to and remodeled over the years...yeah. Eccentric indeed. It bobbed quietly in the water, thumping gently against the dock's bumpers.

The "Police Line Do Not Cross" tape hardly even clashed with the rest of the colors.

I stood looking down at it, simultaneously wishing I had Jen's boldness and wondering what in the world had happened to me that I was even thinking about climbing aboard. What could I possibly find here that the sheriff's deputies hadn't already? And presuming I did so, who would I even tell? It was one thing to trespass on a seemingly abandoned boat; quite another to cross that yellow tape.

"Don't do it," I said to myself in a low whisper.

Then the boat rocked. More vigorously than the movement of the water could possibly explain.

Someone was on that boat!

My heart hammered; my skin tingled painfully; my breath caught, smothering my voice; and I vanished, frozen in place, standing on Lisa's dock right next to a crazy dead man's crazy abandoned boat.

The boat rocked a second time, and I heard the unmistakable sound of footsteps.

I could barely breathe, and I could not move a muscle. My gaze was focused on the boat, right at the opening to the weird little chicken-coop interior.

A woman stepped out onto the deck.

Sheila! I thought, but immediately realized my mistake. It was not her. This woman had none of Sheila's solid posture and blocky build. She was tall and quick; her movements held a certain economy. Her hair was longer, pulled back in a ponytail under a baseball cap. And her eyes, when they gleamed in the starlight, seemed sharp and intelligent.

She reached down and pulled at something on the deck. It bumped and rattled a little. She stopped and waited, alert and still. She made her way to the side of the boat, where two folding chairs had been set up. When the boat shifted and she bumped one of them, she immediately reached out and held it fast, keeping it from toppling over. She glanced up at Lisa's house, obscured by the trees and the steep rise, waiting and listening. Then she bent over and opened something I couldn't see, below my line of vision. A box, or locker, or something.

I remained completely frozen. Only my heart pounded. Even my breath was silent. No matter how much I wanted to run, or scream, my chameleoning kept me in place.

Because that's what had been safest when I was a child. Vanish in place. Make myself invisible and forgotten.

Not so useful now. If I couldn't get it back under control in time for her to leave the boat, she'd walk right into me. Though if I became visible right now, she would see me easily. She was hardly five feet away, and the starlight seemed brighter all the time.

She continued to quietly rummage around the deck, clearly searching for something and not finding it. Her movements went from smooth to forceful, as if she were running out of time. She was going to finish up and leave the boat, jumping off right where I was standing.

What would happen then? Would we both fall into the water? Would she kill me?

Move, limbs, move. I tried to take a deeper breath. I could barely control even that simple a movement.

Suddenly, a fast-moving dark shape flashed at the corner of my vision, on the beach behind me. The woman saw it too. Her head shot up and she stared after whatever it was.

Wasn't she afraid of getting caught trespassing? She was so clearly not any kind of authority, and she'd crossed police line tape to search a dead man's boat. What if she…

She stared at the bushes and dark foliage at the end of Lisa's small beach, where the mystery figure had gone. Animal? Person? I wished I could turn my head.

The woman stepped forward to the front of the boat. It rocked crazily under her weight, but ultimately kept its balance. She stood there, peering into the darkness. I was now completely behind her. *Move it, move it.* Another deep breath.

Nothing more moved on shore. But here, on the dock: my hand moved.

Oh, thank god. I flexed my fingers, as tentatively as possible. After another long moment, my neck released enough so that I could glance down at myself. My eyes still wanted to shy away from myself, but not so badly as before.

I was visible, just a little bit. Both bad and good.

Another breath, and then another, and I felt my legs coming

to life once more. I crouched down, then slowly, quietly, crab-walked myself backwards, moving further out the dock but placing myself near the back of the boat, and—I hoped!—more out of sight.

I was halfway there when the shape moved again, darting back across the beach. And I had to stifle a gasp of relieved amazement.

James, my silly orange cat, was racing around on Lisa Cannon's beach. Probably chasing a shrew or a water rat. My little hunter.

The woman relaxed, seeing his light fur in the starlight. Just a cat, not a person. I was mostly out of her sight. I was pretty sure she wouldn't notice me, hunkered down nearly below the walls of the boat, or whatever they're called. *I really have to improve my nautical knowledge*, I thought nonsensically. If I was going to live on an island, I ought to not sound like a complete land-lubber when I had to describe my totally insane actions down here on the dock.

From my now-lower vantage point, I watched as the stranger on the boat soundlessly hauled herself over its rail onto the dock—right where I had been standing a minute ago. She gave one dark, disgusted look back at the boat and the police tape she'd had to pick her way through, and moved up the dock and across the beach, in the opposite direction from the Brixton estate. She made almost no sound at all. In a minute, she was gone altogether. The only sounds were the tiny waves lapping the shore, and the slowly calming beat of my heart.

My stinging, tingling skin settled down. I became completely visible once more. And I was *really* late getting back home.

I stood up, stretching my stiff muscles, and hurried off the dock. I looked for James as I quickly crossed Lisa's beach to the Brixton beach, but I didn't see him. I thought about calling, but I didn't want to make any noise. He knew where he lived; he'd come home soon, I told myself, as I climbed my home beach and walked up the lawn to the back door of the guesthouse.

I paused on the back stoop, reconnoitering and finishing

calming myself. No one was in the kitchen. Cleanup had been finished, thanks to all my lovely relatives and friends. I smelled something delicious, and saw that the oven was on again: the pies were warming.

I took a moment in the quiet of the night to clear away the last of my mental panic and consider what I'd seen. I'd seen a woman on the deck of a boat that belonged to a man who had apparently died of natural causes the day before, when he was interrupted in the middle of a common household burglary. It wasn't unusual that I'd panicked and chameleoned at the sight of her—she was prowling around where I'd seen a murder not long ago. But, I reminded myself, she was just prowling around. For all I knew, she lived on that boat with Ephraim, or at least knew him. I was guilty of overreaction in the extreme.

There was nothing wrong. I needed to relax, and let the sounds of family lead me back inside.

I followed the sound of voices to the front room, where I found everyone flopped in various states of exhausted stuffed-ness around a crackling fire. "Hey," I said to the room in general, keeping my voice as casual as I could.

"Oh, there you are," Jen said, from the couch where she was sitting by my brother. "We were wondering."

She didn't sound too concerned, though. Which was explained a moment later by my mother's adding, "Yeah, Cam vanishes from time to time."

Kevin gave me a confused look. I turned my head away... catching sight of Colin, who looked adorable, and slightly confused. He had chosen a seat as far across the small room from Kevin as he could get, I noticed. "Yeah," I agreed with my mom. Keeping it vague. "Hey, so the pies smell really good!"

Cliff laughed. "We were going to eat them all ourselves, as payment for doing all the dishes, but your new best friend here pointed out that we shouldn't do that to the hostess."

"Aw, thanks," I said, smiling at Jen. It felt so good, so *normal*, to be here in this comfy room with all these nice people.

Well, most of them. Kevin was still sort of scowling. Then again, who had invited him anyway? If we weren't on a remote island in the Straits of San Juan de Fuca, he could have just driven his stupid Intruder right back home again, couldn't he?

Anyway, the normalcy of the moment stood in stark relief against what had just happened to me. Had I really just seen anything to worry about? A woman poking around on a dead man's boat?

No, don't think that. Don't go there. You're safe now.

"I was looking for the cat, and then I went next door," I said, even though nobody had really asked, exactly.

"To my folks?" JoJo asked. "Why?"

"No," I said, turning to him. "To Lisa's. To see how she was doing."

JoJo was well into his cups—or his bottles—but he blanched a little at this. Clearly, he'd forgotten about Lisa altogether. And about *her* intruder. "Oh."

"She's doing all right," I said to him, and turned to the rest of the room. "My neighbor on that side,"—I pointed—"Lisa Cannon. She had a break-in, and it kind of freaked her out."

"A break-in?" My father sat up, looking all concerned and fatherly. "When?"

"Yesterday," I said. So much for trying to distract everyone from what I'd just seen down at Lisa's dock. "That's why the cop came by earlier, to talk to me."

"Kidnappings and break-ins? I thought this was a quiet, remote island!" my mom said, also looking nearly panicked. "Camille, I think you should move back to Seattle, where it's safe."

I shot a warning look to Kevin, who had brightened at this. He caught sight of my expression and kept his mouth shut. "Mom, it's just a fluke. A big city is way more dangerous than Orcas Island. Besides, Lisa's really rich, and has a spectacular house, and she's been in the news lately, because of—all that. Anyway, the

cops know who broke in. He was…he's a kind of homeless guy."
Yeah, it really wouldn't do to mention that he'd been found dead
on her floor yesterday as well. "We have a super strong sense of
community here." I gestured toward Jen and Colin. "I've already
made such really good friends, and I've only been here a few
weeks. It took me forever to meet anyone in Seattle, and then
they were all snobs and hipsters."

I heard the small sound of Kevin sucking in his breath. Clearly,
what I'd said had struck a nerve. Well, did he think his snooty
foodie friends were *friendly* to me? Always trying to one-up each
other with who had been to what place and which emulsion married with what other flavor and on and on and on about each
little detail of what was on the plate. It had made eating out the
least fun thing I could imagine.

He gave me a pained look, which I ignored.

"Well, your neighbors do seem friendly," Mom allowed. "In
fact, someone came by and left a bag of the world's largest carrots."

"What?" Both Jen and I leaned forward, mouths agape. "Who
brought it?" I asked.

"Oh, I didn't see who it was," Mom said. "But when I went
to take the recycling to the porch, there it was, leaning against
the door." She smiled. "I assumed it was the same person who
brought the zucchini. We can have carrot cake muffins in the
morning!"

"That is too weird," I said. *Dead women don't drop by with carrots, do they?* Jen shook her head, staring back at me. "Who could
be doing this?" I asked.

"You don't know?" Mom asked.

"Sounds like Paige Berry," Colin said. "She's always one for the
strange gifts, right? Has quite a garden. Cold frame and all."

"I've never met Paige Berry," I said. "I hear a lot about her,
though. She must live really close by?"

Colin grinned. "Not far."

I was about to interrogate him further when the timer went off in the kitchen.

"Pie!" Jen leaped to her feet, followed closely by Cliff. My, those two seemed to be hitting it off nicely... Leave it to Jen to become interested in someone who lived on the other side of the world.

"Pie!" JoJo echoed a moment later, then got languidly to his feet and followed them to the kitchen.

"I guess it's dessert time," I said to my parents.

Kevin was still sitting there, looking hurt and defeated. "I don't suppose anybody wants to hear about letting the pies rest and cool off before cutting them. In fruit pies, it gives the pectin a chance to bind—"

"No," I said. "No, we do not."

℞

I don't even know what time it was when we all made it to bed. I just knew that, yet again, it was far too late for me, with how early I'd be waking up, and how little sleep I'd gotten last night.

I was sleeping alone in my bed, which was what I wanted, no matter that Kevin—and maybe even Colin—had other ideas. I had finally taken a look inside that monstrous RV: it was, honest to god, bigger than our Seattle apartment had been. It had two queen-sized beds and twin bunk beds, plus a serious full-on couch, like you'd put in a real house. And armchairs. Several of them. It was the most ridiculous vehicle I'd ever seen. How did all that furniture not just fall all over the place when the thing was being driven?

Anyway, it was kind of a no-brainer that our several unexpected overnight guests would bunk in there. "Seriously?" I'd asked, when I'd helped Cliff carry his stuff into the monstrosity. "People take these things to the wilderness and pretend they're camping?"

"Lap of luxury," Kevin said. "Listen, I have plans for this. I'm ready to live the van life. I'll tell you about it tomorrow." He looked both embarrassed and proud. He was probably getting all sorts of hipster-fodder points out of doing this. Honestly, after a while I'd lost track of the folds of irony required to maintain the hipster lifestyle. It had seemed so important to me once upon a time.

Or maybe I'd been in love.

So I was happy to be sleeping alone. Tonight. Yes, maybe some day again I'd want to share my bed with someone. Maybe some day I'd meet a man who would understand me...in all my eccentricities. My spookiness, my need for sudden alone time. The way I literally vanished when things got challenging.

But for now, this was good.

Although...

And before I could even finish thinking of him, I heard a tiny, interrogative *Prrr-ow*? James leapt up onto my bed.

"You rascal!" I whisper-hissed at him, scratching his ears and rubbing his back. His fur was very cold: he had just come from outside. "How did you even get in here?" My parents weren't still up, were they? Had someone left a door or window open? Or were cats just magical, somehow occupying interstitial spaces in the normal continuum in order to slip through solid walls?

I didn't care. James purred ferociously as I petted him, then pulled him under the covers with me. He liked it under there; he gave only a token protest before settling down in preparation to sleep.

"You're my best buddy ever," I told him, curling around his fuzzy little body. After a few minutes, he started warming up a little. I could use the body heat, even from such a slight little guy. "You saved my life this evening, you know?"

He purred in answer.

"You're the best little bodyguard-cat ever," I murmured, pulling the covers more tightly over both of us. "You saw that spooky lady and distracted her, so I could escape." Not that she was such a threat. It's just, coming from where I did, so many things felt like threats.

His purring slowed and his breathing became slow and regular. In another minute, he was asleep.

Crazy Sheila had given me this cat. She'd appeared at my doorstep one day—before I knew just how crazy she was—and pulled a skinny orange kitten with a white face out of her jacket. *Hey,* she'd said, thrusting the animal at me. *I think you need protection.*

How absurd was that? And yet…little James had done it. He'd kept me safe.

I would need to let Kip know what I'd seen. Probably I should have called him at once; but there was no sense doing it now. The woman, whoever she was, was hours gone, and probably no threat at all. But I would call Kip in the morning. I committed what I had been able to make out of her features to memory, rehearsing what I'd seen to myself, like when you wake up from a vivid dream and want to remember it. It was already seeming less and less real to me. Like a dream.

Speaking of dreams… "Sweet dreams," I whispered to my zonked-out cat, and fell asleep myself.

Friday

CHAPTER 7

I started the first pot of coffee, not worrying about waking folks up. If I was awake, they could darn well be.

Funny how relaxed one gets, just a day or two into houseguests.

I hadn't called Kip yet. Same logic as the middle of the night: the prowler was long gone, and it was early in the morning on the Friday after Thanksgiving. I'd call him midday, maybe. Much longer than that and he would wonder why I'd waited.

I wasn't putting off an uncomfortable conversation. Of course not, not *me*.

Dad wandered into the kitchen after I'd been sitting at the table with a mug of coffee for awhile. "Mmm," he said, pouring himself a cup and adding several teaspoons of sugar.

"You guys sleep well?"

"Sure did. Your mom still is."

"Good for her." Mom always did like to sleep in. If I'd been actually blood-related to her, I'd have wondered where in the world I got my own penchant for rising so early.

"Any word from the boys?" Dad motioned vaguely toward the parking area, where the Intruder remained.

"Nope. It's just you and me, Dad."

We grinned at each other and drank our coffee in comfortable silence for a few minutes. I told myself to enjoy it; it would probably be the last bit of peace I'd have all day.

Why in the world had I thought I wanted a house full of people for five days?

Well, in my defense, I'd just thought I was inviting my parents. All the rest of the gang had sort of...accumulated. At least Jen and Colin had gone back home last night after dessert, and JoJo had returned to the main house. We'd only be five for breakfast, not eight.

Speaking of breakfast... I got up and started rummaging around the kitchen. "We've got bagels," I said.

"Oh, your mother and I wanted to take you all out for breakfast," Dad said. "I forgot to mention. Does the island have a good breakfast place?"

"I'm sure it does," I said, "but there's this bakery..."

And that is how we found ourselves, forty-five minutes later, caravanning to town to descend upon the Brown Bear. I had Cliff in my car; I'd made Mom and Dad drive Kevin in their own. I hadn't invited him here, and I wasn't the least bit interested in spending any alone time with him whatsoever. He'd apparently had no luck getting ferry reservations for that thing he was driving. I'd had no idea the ferries were so restrictive; or maybe it was just because of the reduced schedule for the holiday.

Or maybe he wasn't really trying.

"Thailand is great, but—" Cliff was saying as I pulled up to the stop sign at the intersection of Crow Valley and West Beach Roads. "Wait, what the hell? 'Passing Gas', really?"

I snickered and glanced over at the funky hardware store with its one gas pump. "Yeah. Island humor, I guess."

"Wow." He shook his head.

"You were saying?" I asked. "'Thailand is great, but—'?"

"Oh, right. Baked goods: those are not a tropical thing. That's all I'm saying."

I laughed again, thinking of the Brown Bear's chocolate muffins, their fresh croissants, their quiche, their bread pudding... "You won't be disappointed."

"I never thought I'd want to eat again, after yesterday, but it's the darnedest thing."

"I always wake up starving the day after Thanksgiving." I looked over at my brother, still smiling. It was so good to have him here.

Once we got to town, I had trouble finding a parking place. "Did everyone decide to come into town?" I asked, finally finding a spot almost two blocks inland, in front of the co-op. "I would have thought the traditional pie-for-breakfast rule would have held for more folks."

"Mmm, pie," Cliff said, getting out of the car, then shivering dramatically. "Jeez, I can *not* get used to the temperature here."

"Wimp. It's actually pretty nice today." And it was: the sun was making another appearance, and the temperature had to be approaching fifty. Balmy.

We hiked back down the street to the bakery, only to find it overflowing with customers. The line was out the door and folks filled the outdoor seating area. Mom and Dad and Kevin joined us a minute later, having parked even farther afield. We shuffled slowly from foot to foot as we waited. It felt like trying to go out to brunch in Seattle. I hadn't missed this one bit.

"I hope they have anything left by the time we get in the door," I grumbled.

Kevin was scrolling through something on his phone, clearly taking advantage of the stronger wireless signal here in town. "Huh, pretty good ratings," he said. "Apparently the chocolate muffin is a specialty. I wonder how it holds up to, say, the kouign-amann at Bakery Nouveau in Capitol Hill."

I felt myself bristle with annoyance. "They're astonishing," I said through clenched teeth. "Like nothing I've ever had before."

My brother nudged me discreetly in the ribs with an elbow. "Relax, sis," he whispered.

"I need a moment," I said to the group, and walked away from them, crossing the street to the sound-side. I walked past the bookstore and the pub. Eventually, the buildings ended and I could see the water.

I knew I shouldn't let Kevin get under my skin like that. But he was such a pretentious ass! And I'd known that, from day one, but I hadn't let myself see it, or believe it. Now, everything I'd repressed was just busting out all over. I couldn't stop it.

Why did he have to come here? And why couldn't he just put his know-it-allness down for even a day? And why did his eyes have to be such a beautiful shade of green? I glanced back over at the bakery; I could barely see the four of them, but enough to know they were still nowhere near the door. Kevin still had his nose in his phone.

Which reminded me. I might as well take advantage of the strong cell signal here in town too, as well as this unexpected moment of privacy. I pulled out my phone and touched Kip's number.

"Good morning, Camille." He sounded pleased, though entirely unsurprised, to hear from me. "How was your feast?"

"It was great," I said. "Very feasty. But I'm calling on business."

"Oh?" I could almost see his smile fade and his cop-face reassert itself. "What's up?"

"I, um, saw something last night." Now I wished I'd rehearsed this phone call a bit, or at least thought about what I was going to say. *Just tell him what you saw, fool.* "I went to visit Lisa and I walked home by the water and I saw that fellow's boat, with the police tape around it, and there was a woman on it, and she was looking for something." The words came out in a rushed blur. When I'd finished, I glanced around me, but I was still alone. My family and Kevin had advanced a little closer to the bakery door.

"Wait a minute, Camille, slow down. Say that all again."

I went through it more coherently this time, reassuring Kip that she hadn't seen me, that I was unharmed, that I didn't know who she was, that she had left the beach. "She was heading west, I guess—down beach, away from our houses." And then I had to explain why I'd waited twelve or more hours to call. "I didn't have my phone on me," I told him, even though I couldn't actually remember if that was true or not. "And by the time I was home, she was long gone."

"Long gone doesn't mean we couldn't have found her more easily if we'd started looking last night," he said. "The notion of trails going cold doesn't just apply to the movies, Camille."

"I'm sorry. I was exhausted and I just wanted to sleep." I kicked at a small stone on the sidewalk. "But I'm telling you now. And I don't have much time, I'm with my folks and…I didn't want to scare them with this. And it just didn't seem like a big deal."

"I understand. I'll want to get a better description of her, though, and the rest of a statement from you. Will you be able to get to town any time today?"

"I'm in town now," I told him, glancing down the street again. "And I've got to go—everyone's at the door of the Brown Bear."

Kip chuckled. Ah, such a golden voice. He really did miss his calling, going into law enforcement and not radio work. "Can you stop by the station after the bakery?"

I started to say no, but then realized I could send my brother home in my folks' car. Tell them all I was doing a little shopping or something, and that I needed some time alone. They'd understand. "Sure. An hour?"

"Perfect. I'll see you then."

I walked back to my family (and the interloper), joining them just as they sidled into the tiny bakery, squeezing past hordes of people leaving clutching paper bags and the few—very lucky—folks who were hogging the indoor seats. I smiled to myself as I noticed Kevin's rapt interest in the display case, and how hard he was working to disguise said interest. It smelled astonishingly good in here, and I was suddenly twice as starving, as though I hadn't eaten at all yesterday.

Or as though I'd eaten so much, I'd stretched my stomach to double its normal capacity, and all that capacity yawned empty now, needing refilling.

In any event, I was excited to be here. And glad that I'd gotten a few minutes away from my annoyance. And gladdest of all to see four gleaming chocolate muffins in their paper bases on a platter in the front case!

❦

It was easy enough to send everyone home with the promise to follow, after my errand. They were so full of delicious baked goods that their brains were short-circuited. Nobody thought to question what I could possibly need to do or buy in town.

I drove out to the sheriff's substation on Mount Baker Road, parking next to the never-used SUV-ambulance hybrid thing. Obviously just part of the scenery, or decoration. Or, heck, maybe they did actually use it as an ambulance. Just because my friends had rescued me and taken me to Jen Darling's house when I'd been kidnapped and shot didn't mean this never got called out.

I got out of my car and rang the doorbell. No response; I glanced at my watch. It had been nearly an hour since I'd called Kip; obviously he wasn't here yet.

I paced around the parking lot, remembering my first time coming here, when I'd still thought of Kip as Deputy Rankin. When I'd thought that sheriff's offices were always open, with receptionists and all that. All those many…days ago. I hadn't been here that long at all. I smiled to myself, marveling again at how quickly Orcas Island had begun to seem like home. How foreign the outside world—"America"—seemed already.

Within a few minutes, Kip's cruiser pulled into the parking lot. This time, he parked out here, not going into the garage. "Hello, Camille. Thanks for coming in," he said, giving me his million-dollar smile as he unlocked the station's door.

"My pleasure."

"I'm glad you can find the time, today. I thought with all your guests, you might be overwhelmed."

"Oh, I'm definitely overwhelmed." That made us both laugh a little.

"Are you finding time to work on your play?"

Had everyone on the island heard about my play?

I blushed and shook my head. "I haven't had any time to write."

He smiled. "I hope you'll get back to it. I'm so looking forward to seeing your work."

I had no idea what to say, but I was definitely pleased by that idea, myself.

He breathed in and out his nose sharply, as if clearing out the last of his non-professional pleasantries. "Let's get this over with, shall we?"

"Please," I said. I was so tired of talking to Kip in a professional capacity.

After the traditional offer-and-refusal of coffee or anything else to drink, he got us both settled in the little interview room and pulled out his notebook and recorder. "Okay. Perhaps you could run through the sequence of events again for me. Starting with why you were next door to begin with last night?" He blinked, calm as glass.

I bristled at once. "Lisa Cannon is my neighbor and friend," I said, irritation in my voice. "I was worried about her; I went by to see how she was doing. Isn't that a *normal* thing to do when someone's had a traumatic event? To care how they *are*?"

"Let's de-escalate this, Cam." Kip raised his hands placatingly. "I'm not accusing you of anything; I just need to get the full picture painted here. You went to check on your friend: that's quite enough for me."

Great. I was overreacting. Now I got to feel ridiculous, too. I took a deep breath and de-escalated myself. "I also kind of needed to get out of the house," I added, just to give him something more. "It's a lot of people for a small house."

"I expect so."

We shared a smile. Mine was kind of sheepish. "Okay. So. After I left Lisa's, it was really dark, and I didn't want to walk back through the path in the woods. I knew our beaches connected, so I thought I'd go down that way." *Don't ask how I know our beaches are connected.* It was a reasonable thing to know, about one's next-door neighbor. Right? Of course. Kip and I had first met when I'd seen something when I'd gone walking on the Brixtons' beach, after all.

He led me through a full recounting of the event, making copious notes when I got to the description. "She was a woman. It was dark, and hard to see much detail. But it wasn't Sheila."

He glanced up at this.

"Definitely not Sheila," I added. "She moved so much more—gracefully and quickly. Have you...found Sheila?"

"No body has been recovered," he allowed.

I shivered a little. "I really wanted to think she was dead."

"We're assuming so, but until a body is found..."

"Right."

"So," he prompted, "older or younger than Sheila?"

"Maybe a few years older."

"What did she look like?"

"Well, kind of slim. She moved carefully, like an athlete. Long hair in a ponytail, bright eyes." I thought further, trying to express just what had struck me about her. "She didn't appear to be any of the actors I've met. I mean, they run together, but she seemed older and quieter than any of the troupe. More, I don't know, professional."

"I see."

"She was really cautious, Kip. Economy of movement cautious."

Kip raised one eyebrow. "Economy of movement. I see."

I felt myself faintly blushing. I knew it wasn't much of a physical description, but maybe it would ring some bells with Kip, or with other local law enforcement. Clearly they'd been familiar with Ephraim Snooks. "Is this helping at all?" I asked.

"A little. What about hair color, eye color? Clothing?"

"It was dark." I struggled to remember exactly, and gave him what I could. Her eyes had been bright, but in the dark, I hadn't been able to make out their color, or even thought to try, frankly. "I'm sorry. I was sort of…not believing it."

"Of course not." Kip continued to scribble notes.

"Kip, what does it mean?" I asked, frustrated. "Why does stuff keep happening around me—around Lisa? Is there some…larger thing I don't know about?"

"I am quite certain that there are many things you don't know about. On Orcas Island or elsewhere. But this is an active investigation, and…"

"You're really going there?" I asked with a brave smile, trying to cover my own unease with a joke. "You can't tell me anything?"

He gave me a gentle smile back. "Camille, I always tell you everything I can, and everything you need to know. So what I will say to you now is: if the woman didn't see you, and didn't come near your place, and didn't threaten you in any way—leave any notes, or gifts—then I'd say you have nothing to worry about."

I suddenly remembered the newest vegetable gifts, the zucchini and the carrots. Should I mention those? Colin had said that sounded like Paige Berry. Was she ever going to actually introduce herself, or just sneak around with produce? The fond, relaxed way people talked about her, she clearly wasn't a threat to my world.

At least, I didn't think so.

"What is it?" Kip asked, expertly reading my open book of a face.

"Oh…nothing. I just remembered something I have to get at the grocery store." I flashed him a helpless smile. "For, you know, lunch." My cheeks started to go a brighter pink.

"You don't have any leftovers?"

I shrugged, smiled. God, I was the world's worst liar. Well, it served him right, didn't it? If he wasn't going to tell me anything,

I could show him the same courtesy.

He watched me for another long moment before nodding. "All right. Well, you let me know if you think of anything else. And thank you again for coming in, and for all the information."

"Thank you for being here," I said, getting to my feet and picking up my bag.

I drove slowly back toward the estate, thinking about everything. It was obviously not a coincidence that stuff kept happening around Lisa's house, around the Brixton estate. We'd been in the news; that attracted attention. Whatever Sheila had actually been up to, she obviously hadn't been acting alone. Even with the mysterious Gregory Baines dead, there were clearly others involved.

Had Ephraim Snooks been one of those others? Kip, and Lisa, had imagined that he'd just been acting opportunistically. And maybe that was true. But the woman searching Snooks's boat…she had been far more purposeful. She wasn't just some near-homeless rando looking for loot, or drugs. She was looking for something specific…and not finding it.

She'd be back. I knew she would.

I had to stay away from the beach.

☙

Except that when I got back home, *everyone* was on the beach.

I had a bad moment when I walked in and found the guesthouse empty, but quickly followed the sounds of voices and laughter down across the lawn and down the hill.

My parents were sitting on folding chairs; Kevin and Cliff were perched on the community dock (Cliff sprawled comfortably; Kevin had on absurdly tight and skinny jeans which kept him from sitting cross-legged, so he was sort of posing as he reclined), and everyone was watching a bunch of strangers argue and cavort.

No, not strangers: Lisa's actors, the ones I'd met when I'd

shown up for happy hour a week or two ago. Though I couldn't remember all their names. Lisa stood off to the edge with a small frown, holding a script that had been folded and refolded till it was nearly fraying.

Cliff spotted me and leapt up. "Mealy! You never told me you had a production company next door! This is fascinating! And they're going to do your play this summer? Why didn't you *tell* me?"

Lisa shot me an apologetic smile as she walked toward me. "I didn't mean to speak out of turn about your play. It's just that we're all so excited about it."

I shook my head. "I only hope I can deliver."

"Oh, she'll deliver, all right," said Cliff, suppressing a smile. "I'll make sure of it, I'll supervise all the way from Thailand."

Great. I had to change the subject. "I'm wondering if Diana will freak out with all these people on her beach?"

Lisa gave me a gracious smile. "I'm not really trespassing; JoJo used to let us rehearse down here when we needed more room than my beach."

"Oh, gosh, well," I said. "If the Brixtons don't—"

"I suppose we can ask them," Lisa said, glancing behind me.

Diana Brixton tottered down the hillside in too-high heels. Because any heels were too high to maneuver down a muddy lawn like this. But just try telling Diana Brixton anything. At the moment, her face was screwed up into a pained scowl—an expression that was wiped away at once and replaced with a saccharine smile as soon as she caught sight of Lisa.

Interesting, I thought. I knew they weren't bosom buddies, but...

"Oh, Lisa, it's you," said Diana. "I didn't know *what* was going on down here."

The actors—five of them, I now saw—were all standing around, waiting for their director to pay attention to them again. My dad waved and smiled at Diana, clearly enjoying whatever show was being put on for him, whether a rehearsal or interpersonal drama.

"Oh, my apologies, Diana," Lisa said, smooth as ever. "Joseph has let us rehearse here; I know I should have come and asked you directly, but I didn't want to impose."

"Not an imposition at all!" Diana said, holding tight to her smile. "Emmett and I are huge supporters of the arts, as of course are Joseph and Clarice. It's an absolute privilege to be able to support them so *directly* like this." She now glanced around at the rest of us. Her eyes lit on me. "Camille? May I have a word?"

"Of course." What did she think I was going to be able to do about any of this? But she was my boss, so I walked over to her. I followed as she withdrew up the hill a bit.

We weren't exactly out of earshot when she said, "Is that...recreational vehicle going to be staying much longer? It's blocking the entirety of your parking."

Which affects you how? I thought; and it wasn't even true, we'd noodled the cars out to get to the bakery this morning. But I said, "I am so sorry, Mrs. Brixton. You know I didn't invite him. And I guess he's having trouble getting ferry reservations. It's the holiday weekend, and..."

"I know that. But there are campgrounds on the island. Has he checked any of those?"

I broke into a grin. "Campgrounds! What a marvelous idea." Why hadn't I thought of it? "I don't know, but I'll get right on it. Thank you!"

She eyed me somewhat suspiciously. I guess she'd expected me to act like a sheepish employee, not a thankful one. To beg for Kevin to stay. Ha. She briskly nodded her head. "Good. I'll look forward to its departure, then."

"As will I. I can't *wait* until that thing is out of here."

Still grinning, I headed back to join the others. "What's up?" my brother asked.

I settled on the dock next to him, on the other side of Kevin.

"I'll tell you later," I muttered, giving him a *not here* sibling-glance.

"Ahhhhh," Cliff said. "Got it."

Lisa had already started the actors on their scene again. I didn't know what this play was supposed to be about, but this particular scene involved a loud argument and some fake fisticuffs. Hence all the laughter I'd heard: in their efforts to not actually injure one another, they were dancing around, swinging wildly, and collapsing into hysterics at how absurd it all looked. One of the women kept insisting, "I am the fight choreographer, and what I say goes!" She was roundly ignored by the men. Lisa was clearly about to lose patience with them all; the actors—three men and two women—were getting punch-drunk, goofing off harder each time. I certainly hoped they didn't plan on any fight choreography in my play. Hairdressers rarely resorted to fistfights. Except...that could be fun, couldn't it?

"Maybe we shouldn't be watching?" I whispered to Cliff.

"No, she wanted us here," he told me. "They do better with an audience, she said. Keeps them more focused."

"This is *more* focused?"

"Well..." He grinned as another pratfall went horribly awry, sending a man and the non-choreographer woman tumbling to the ground in a jumble of limbs and giggles.

"I'm so sorry!" cried the woman through her laughter. "Maybe we should take a little break?"

"I think that's probably for the best," Lisa said, snapping her script shut and pinching the bridge of her nose between two delicate fingers. "God knows I need one." She turned and walked down the beach toward her own property...and the police-taped boat.

It was broad daylight. She'd be fine. And her body language made it perfectly clear that she didn't want anyone following her.

"Well, show's over, I guess," Dad said, getting up out of his folding chair.

"Aw, did I miss it?" We all turned to see JoJo tripping down the hillside, followed by Colin. Colin? What was he doing here? JoJo looked mildly amused. "Mom came back on a tear about something, I just had to come down and check it out."

"Hey," I said to them both as I got up. "They're just taking a break. Right?" I looked over at the actors, who were huddled over another copy of the script, still giggling and snorting and elbowing each other. Ignoring us all completely. Well, actors are supposed to pretend like the audience doesn't exist, right?

"Tried calling, but nobody answered," Colin said, leaning against the railing of the dock next to me and Cliff. "Driving back from Deer Harbor, thought I'd drop by and say thanks for the grub yesterday."

"Huh." I pulled out my phone, but I only had one bar of service. No missed calls. (None that had shown up yet, anyway.) "My pleasure! I was glad you could join us."

JoJo had already produced another folding chair from somewhere and pulled it up next to my dad's, who sat back down again. They quickly began an energetic conversation about the Mariners. Funny, JoJo hadn't struck me as a sports fan. Though I'd only known him a day or so before my folks arrived. But he was clearly super into it, and his enthusiasm was infectious. Even Mom was leaning in, looking interested. Well, JoJo was easy on the eyes. And Mom was not blind.

Smiling and shaking my head, I turned back to the guys sitting on the dock with me. Kevin still sat a little apart from us all, looking out of place. Well, he should: he *was* out of place. As soon as I got back up to the house, I'd look up campgrounds for him.

Or ferry reservations.

A slight breeze picked up, and my stomach growled. Seriously? I couldn't possibly be hungry again.

But the house was full of leftovers...

"Hey, who wants a turkey sandwich?" I asked.

እ⌒

My phone beeped with voice mails when I got back up to the house—by myself. Somehow, I'd let myself get volunteered into making sandwiches for the whole gang. Including the actors. How did this happen?

At least I got myself some alone time. Even my wayward cat was off gallivanting somewhere.

As I sliced turkey off the bone and spread mayo across a whole bunch of bread, I listened to the messages. There was one from Kip, from before I'd met him in town; one from Colin, basically a repeat of what he'd said in person; one from Jen, thanking me for the meal yesterday and not-so-subtly wondering if we needed any help with the leftovers; and then one from Lisa, from just a few minutes ago.

I perked up as I listened to it, setting the mayonnaisey knife down on the counter.

"Cam, I'm sorry to bother you, but…I'm wondering if you could come over real quick? I know you've got your family there, but I need…another set of eyes. Thanks."

I stood holding the phone, swallowing this latest rush of adrenaline. Lisa needed me? Oh please, let there not be any bodies involved this time.

CHAPTER 8

I was still holding the phone, staring at it blankly, when a presence at the back door made me look up, startled. "Kevin!"

"Cam?" His green eyes were shining with hope.

I unfroze. "I started making sandwiches and then I got a call, I need to run next door real quick. Can you finish?"

His eyes really started to shine, then. "That's why I came up here. I made some special chutneys for just this purpose. And I brought some rustic breads from that new bakery on Capitol Hill. Just leave it all there, I'm on it."

There was a flash, then, when I remembered that Kevin wasn't completely insufferable. He was devoted and passionate about food because he loved it. And he'd been devoted and passionate about other things, too.

Time to blush. Could he tell what I was thinking?

I left before he returned with his loaves and chutneys. The last thing I wanted to feel was confusion about Kevin. He'd had his chance. I'd told him the truth about my chameleoning, and he'd freaked out. He'd called me disturbed and delusional. That was the only chance he would ever have to break my heart. I told myself that yet again as I navigated the muddy path between the estates.

A few minutes later, I stood in Lisa's living room, holding the now-traditional glass of ridiculously exquisite wine. The room itself had also been restored to perfection, all beautiful wood and expensive objets d'art, the windows looking out on Massacre Bay, the floors gleaming. "I'm sorry to bother you, Cam. You must be overwhelmed with all this hospitality."

My alarm lessened as I laughed out loud. "You have no idea how...*stretched* I feel. Except, maybe you do. My family isn't a troupe of actors, but sometimes it feels that dramatic."

It was her turn to laugh. Lisa's laugh was like snow in the Pacific Northwest; rare and beautiful, so it felt special.

"Well, I'm afraid I've asked you here for something that might stretch you a little further. It has to do with the burglary."

My ears pricked up like James's. "So it was a burglary?"

"Yes. After you left, Kip emptied that pillowcase. And it was a strange lot of goods, actually. I wasn't surprised by the drugs. Some ancient painkillers from dental surgery, and I had a bout of insomnia last year, so there was Xanax. He found the spare cash I have on hand here for emergencies—I hide it *very* well, so that surprised me. It was like he knew where it was, to be honest."

"Hm." I didn't like the sound of that.

Lisa continued. "That was, well, pretty much all he had in there, aside from my laptop. Kip let me keep that and the cash, but he took the rest of it in as evidence, which I find absurd. Is he planning to charge a dead man with breaking and entering?"

She had a point. "Is that all Ephraim took?" I caught myself. "Tried to take?"

"Hm. Well, and bathroom things, like soap and deodorant, first aid supplies. He didn't take my iPod. I wonder if he didn't know what it was. The people who live on their boats, they tend to be hermits, somewhat out of touch. A little clannish. But this is the part of it that I hate talking about. He had some of my undergarments in there."

"Oh my gosh! He stole your *underwear*?" I couldn't help myself, I snorted with horrified laughter.

"Isn't that *grotesque*?" Lisa was laughing, too. It was such a relief, laughing. We settled down, and Lisa's face knitted in concern. "It's just—well, I hardly know how to say this. I discovered today that something else is missing. Something of vital importance."

And the warmth went out of me, replaced with worry. "What is it?"

Lisa gave a deep sigh that somehow maintained its delicacy. "It's hard to explain. I guess because...well...Cam. I hope you won't think less of me for what I'm about to tell you. Very few people know this. I'm trusting you."

I felt myself warming again. Whatever fears I'd had about becoming friends with someone of Lisa's, well, her stature, she had faith in me. "You can trust me."

"I think I can." She took a sip of her wine, then set it aside and looked searchingly into my eyes. "Have you ever been divorced?"

"No, I'm too..." I'd been about to say I was too young, but at twenty-seven, I really wasn't. "I'm not ready for marriage. I'm still working out some basic things about myself. So, no. I haven't."

"I don't recommend it. It doesn't bring out the best in people." She breathed in through her nose, let it out, shook her head. "I was married to the man of my dreams for years. I was so proud of my marriage." She shook her head again. "It came to my attention that he had betrayed me horribly. Repeatedly. I had no idea, of course, but when the truth came out, it became clear that my entire marriage was a sham, just something he'd let me believe in while he lived a secret life. And the ridiculous part is, he didn't want a divorce. He was perfectly satisfied. He thought the answer was for me to...accept who he was. He said this was my fault, for not understanding him. He blamed me. I believe he is a sociopath."

I shuddered with hatred for this man I had never met.

"I offered him a generous settlement just to get things over with, but he wanted more. He had his own assets, his own company, he needed nothing from me to live a very comfortable life. He was doing it, I believe, in order to punish me for ending things. He drove me to despair. I think…" She stared out the window. "I actually *know* that he wanted me to kill myself. He would have had everything, then."

Just the thought of this made my blood boil. Who could have done this to Lisa? Who would hurt her? I looked at her sitting here, her fine bone structure, her graceful hands, sitting in her perfectly elegant home clothed in something simple and unassuming, even though she had all the money in the world. She was so kind and gracious. I'd never met her ex, but I hated him.

"I didn't, obviously. The divorce dragged on. He decided that he wanted half of my business, so I sold it. It became necessary to make certain assets unavailable in order to protect the monetary proceeds from my life's work. He actually hired a team of forensic accountants. They were extremely expensive, and cost him more than they were able to uncover. My team was better." Her eyes gleamed with the ghost of a smile. "It was my only revenge for what he put me through."

"If I were you I'd have…" I'd have what? Killed him? "I don't think it was enough."

She lifted one shoulder in a delicate shrug. "He cared an awful lot about money and prestige. The divorce cost him both. It was the best I could do, as far as revenge or payback or whatever you want to call it. Which brings us to what's missing. Most of these records are too sensitive to trust to computers alone. These files are deeply encrypted, but it's tricky. There is a binder that holds a key amount of recovery data to make sure I can always access my assets. I keep the binder in a safe that's anchored to this house's foundation. Three people have the combination to that safe, which involves fingerprint verification. That binder is missing, Cam. And I think it's on Ephraim's boat."

I couldn't prevent the gasp from escaping me. Lisa's eyes focused on me, sharply. "You know something," she said.

"I…saw someone. On his boat. Last night."

"Someone else is looking for my binder?" Lisa leaned forward and poured more wine in my glass. "Tell me everything."

I did. And she didn't even ask me why I hadn't told her sooner. She just blithely assumed I'd sneak onto the boat and look around, find the binder, return it to her.

Well, given everything she'd told me, how could I not?

We agreed that I should do it at night. The boat wasn't going anywhere, at least not today; the cover of darkness would make everything easier. Besides, I had to get back to my own house and deal with all this company. Surely Kevin had had ample time to make even the most artisanal of sandwiches by now. The wine had staved off my hunger a bit, but now that I thought about those sandwiches...

"I'll sneak out tonight and do it," I assured Lisa.

She set down her empty wine glass, rose to her feet, and pulled me into a gentle hug. "Oh, Cam. I will be forever in your debt."

And now I felt warmest of all, deep inside.

ల

My guesthouse was crammed. Everyone who had been on the beach—even the actors—had crowded into the kitchen to grab one or two or six of Kevin's tiny, overstuffed sandwiches. And apparently Jen had taken it upon herself to just come over, since I hadn't called her back.

Kevin had also managed to whip up a batch of turkey-skin cracklins, a platter of zucchini-feta fritters, and an olive oil cole-slaw with shishito peppers and fig balsamic vinegar. Where did he even *get* half these things, I wondered, as I crunched into a cracklin. That Intruder must have plenty of kitchen storage space.

"I understand you're broken up," Jen said to me around a mouthful of fritter. We had maneuvered ourselves out of the kitchen and into the front room, where she'd stoked up the fire. But it was really no less crowded out here, as everyone filled up a plate and followed us. "What I don't understand is how you're not five hundred pounds. Does he cook like this all the time?"

I nodded and swallowed, watching him across the room. He stood by the fire talking to my mom. She must have complimented the slaw, because he was carefully listing all the ingredients to her, and the proportions, and the timing. Completely in his element, completely sincere. Kevin wasn't really such a horrible man, after all. "Pretty much."

Jen shook her head. "I mean, it's great, but wow, single-minded much? He was talking about saffron earlier. About going to four different stores all across the greater Seattle area looking for this specific one—Manga, or something, I don't know—the only good kind, you're totally wasting your time on anything else, might as well be eating lawn clippings…" She rolled her eyes and grinned.

"Mongra," I blurted out before I could stop myself. "It's Mongra saffron, or Lacha, they're the best…" I could feel my cheeks heating. Was I seriously defending my food-obsessed ex-boyfriend? Could I actually tell the difference between Mongra and Aquilla saffrons?

Well, if I was being entirely honest with myself, yes, I could.

Jen was still watching me, waiting for the punch line. Waiting for me to laugh with her at this absurdity. I shrugged. "It's his thing, I guess. He's like a super-taster—well, not literally, but he's more like a super-discerner. He can take a bite of something and figure out all the flavors. And then decide what might make it even better."

She looked at me a moment longer, then took a bite of slaw. "I guess it's good he's in the business he's in, then."

"Yep."

"Are the two of you really through?"

I looked straight in her eyes. "We are one hundred percent through."

Jen lifted one eyebrow and took another bite. Well, she might think Kevin was ridiculous, but it didn't stop her from gobbling down his food. Didn't stop any of us. We finished our lunches in silence, watching everyone else eat and gab. What was the awkward silence about? I hoped I hadn't offended my new friend by defending Kevin.

He wasn't completely ridiculous. And the sandwiches were wonderful. "Jen? Something weird happened last night."

"Weird?" She perked right up. "Tell."

I told her as quietly as I could about looking for James the night before, and seeing someone on Ephraim Snooks's boat. She was, of course, fascinated.

"I wish I'd been with you," she whispered, her eyes dancing with the prospect of solving a mystery. I breathed a tiny sigh of relief as she whispered, "I know every person on this island. I could have told you who she was."

"What if she wasn't from here?"

"No one would set foot on that boat without a reason. It looks like it's on the verge of being swamped." She had a point. So who was it? And what was the mysterious intruder looking for?

"What's all the whispering about?" Cliff had wandered into the living room, and when we wouldn't tell him, he joined the conversation in front of the fire between Kevin and Mom. Cliff had always liked Kevin, so it shouldn't surprise me that they still connected. I'd heard them talking earlier in the day about Thai street cart food, and the restaurateur in Portland who made a name for himself by importing it to America. At decidedly non-street-cart prices, of course.

Even so, if my brother came all the way here from Thailand and spent all his time talking to my ex, that was going to seriously piss me off. I set my empty plate on the side table and turned to Jen just as Kevin raised his voice and said, "Oh, Cam, I want you to hear this too."

She shrugged, her eyes sparkling with mischief. "What now? Locally sourced earthworms for your garden, so your tomatoes will be ever so much more authentic?"

"Shut up," I whispered, mock-punching her in the arm as I got up and joined the group by the fire. Jen followed right behind me.

"I actually wasn't a hundred percent honest with you about the RV," he said, looking into my eyes.

"What?"

How did he manage to look both proud and contrite at the same time? "I didn't just rent it…and it wasn't the only thing available. I, well, I'm kind of renting-to-own."

"What?" I said again, taking a small step back. Colin, chatting with my dad and JoJo by the front door, glanced up at my tone. From the kitchen I heard another shriek of actor-laughter. "Where are you going to *park* that thing in Seattle?"

Kevin looked even prouder, and a bit less contrite. "Well that's just it. The beauty of it. I've given up the apartment. I'm going to totally gut and renovate the Intruder's kitchen and, well, take this show on the road." He gestured to the roomful of people enthusiastically gobbling down his food. People who should not be the least bit hungry. Myself included.

"On the road?" I echoed, confused. "What show?"

Now he smiled broadly. "A traveling restaurant, of course! The Rolling Gourmet, or Kev's Kitchen, or—well, here's where I need help, I don't know what to call it. You're so good with words. You were always talking about writing that screenplay—"

"I *am* writing it," I interrupted. "Only it's a stage play now, and Lisa Cannon wants to make it part of her summer season." *And you'd know all that if you were still in my life*, I thought. *Or were even paying attention earlier, to anything besides food.*

"Perfect! You can write on the road as we travel between cities—"

"Wait, what?"

Now Colin stepped away from his conversation and joined ours, coming to stand protectively close to me. Which again made me both pleased and pissed. I took a half-step away from him, which of course only brought me closer to Kevin.

"And don't worry about the money! I've got it all covered. Mom and Dad are investing, so that's part of it." His grin was ear to ear; I had never seen him so happy. Not even…in our earliest days. And of course his parents would invest. Two college professors who lived on the lake in the Madrona neighborhood. They had *plenty* of money to bankroll their only son in a vanity project like this. "I need your help, though, Cam. To make it all happen."

"I have a job." I waved around the room. "Here: this is my job. I'm the caretaker for two houses and…*acres* of land. I don't need to worry about money." *Well, not much,* I thought, remembering the island's prices.

Kevin blustered on, obviously not even listening to me. The whole room was watching him, rapt. "I got funding from the Grub Network to film a pilot. We'll travel the country on reality TV! You can write the scripts."

I shrunk back, leaning fully into Colin now and not caring. "You are…KIDDING me," I whispered.

"Reality TV doesn't have scripts," JoJo put in from across the room, not even trying to hold back his smirk.

"I need you, Cam. When you left, I…I got kind of lost. I realized how much a part of my life you've become. We're a team. Please come back, please come with me. It'll be great—a huge adventure, so much better than hiding out on a stupid little island at the edge of nowhere." Suddenly, as if this moment couldn't get any more uncomfortable, Kevin dropped to his knees in front of me. He reached into his pocket and pulled out a little white box. "Cam, I miss you. I need you. I want you to marry me."

I was seriously going to faint from embarrassment.

I felt Colin's gentle hands on my upper arms. "Didn't hear 'love' anywhere in that little speech," he grumbled.

"Right." I took a deep breath and stared down at Kevin, who was poised to open that little box, and I would *die* if he opened that little box. "Get up. Don't do this here, now." It was a good thing I was angry enough, because I was also so mortified, I could feel my arms begin to tingle. *No no no*, I told myself. Where was my beer?

Kevin withdrew the box, but stayed on his knees. He reached up and grabbed one of my hands. "No, Cam, it *has* to be now, it *has* to be here. In front of everyone who cares about you." He glanced around the room; my parents, my brother, my friends were all just staring back at him, as dumbfounded as I was. "We were great together, weren't we?" he asked them. "Cliff, you tell her."

My brother opened his mouth and shut it again, slowly shaking his head. "Dude, I like you, but, seriously. This is life. Not reality TV."

Colin's hands on my arms tightened a bit, thankfully avoiding the injury. "Kevin? Maybe give this all a rest right now. Give the lady some space."

Space. Oh yes, that would be a really good thing. "Yes," I breathed out. "I need to…" I pulled out of Colin's arms and stepped past Kevin, intending to head for my bedroom. A few minutes snuggling my cat: that's what I needed.

"Cam!" Kevin cried out, struggling to his feet and grabbing my arm, right over the bandage.

"Ouch!"

Colin, my dad, and my brother all moved to grab Kevin, but it was Jen who actually made contact, slugging him in his skinny shoulder. "Let her go! What's the matter with you!?"

Kevin dropped my arm and howled, though she couldn't possibly have hurt him. Probably he was just surprised that a girl would actually hit him. I stood, now frozen as usual, trying to bully my own body into moving…and staying visible till I could escape. I could see the doorway to the hall, my bedroom door just beyond it…so close, and a thousand miles away.

No one else was frozen, of course. Colin stepped right up into Kevin's face, all angry, aggressive male. (Which only made it worse for me.) "I think it's time for you to leave, friend," he said.

Kevin gave me a panicked look. "Cam! He's wrong, I do love you! You know I do!"

I could not move, I could not speak. My arms tingled. I think I was still visible...god I hoped so. I could only stare back at them all.

"Out," Colin demanded, reaching for Kevin. My ex-boyfriend scrabbled back, then turned for the front door.

"Fine!" he said, his voice high and breaking a little. "I'll go— I'll just—go—" Then he fled out the door. A half-minute later, the sound of the Intruder's massive engine rumbling to life broke the freeze my chameleoning held on me, and I too fled, for the safety and privacy of my bedroom.

"James," I whispered, looking around for him. I'd thought for sure he'd be hiding in here too, away from all the company. Social creature that he might be, this crowd was surely too much for him, even before the yelling started. But he was nowhere. No matter: my bed was here, and that was all I needed. I dove onto it and burrowed under the covers, shivering with relief. I could still hear everyone talking out in the living room, and even the actors in the kitchen had finally figured out that something was going on, and gone to investigate.

Let them, let them all talk and wonder and worry, without me. I let the voices tumble unheeded out there. I didn't have to deal with it, not right now.

"Well, I know what we need," I heard Jen's voice over the rest of them, followed by the sound of a cork leaving a wine bottle. Ever the bartender.

I buried my head deeper under the covers.

$\mathcal{C}\mathcal{D}$

I must have slept, because suddenly it was dark. I stretched and pushed the covers off carefully, so as not to poke any sleeping cats.

But there were none.

"I know you can walk through walls," I muttered to the absent James as I got up and switched on a lamp. I needed to make sure I was at least marginally presentable.

I frowned into the mirror. My clothes were rumpled, though not awful, and my hair was mussed—not artfully, like Lisa's; there was just really no way to cut my tangled mop that would stand up to mashing it into a pillow for a few hours.

Grabbing some mousse off my dresser, I worked it through my dry hair, then studied myself again. It would have to do.

I paused at my bedroom door, listening. I heard quieter voices in comfortable conversation: my folks, Jen, and Cliff, it sounded like. Had everyone else left? That would be nice.

"Hey," Colin said, as soon as I stepped into the living room. He was sitting right next to Kip. Oh well.

"Hey," I said to them both, as Jen leaned over and picked up a bottle of wine just as the lights all went out.

"Oh no!" Mom cried. "I just turned the oven on to heat up some pie—did we blow a fuse?"

"I'll go find out," I heard Dad say.

A sharp beam of light sliced through the room: Kip, of course, with his monster cop flashlight. "I'll go check with you, Adam," he said, authoritatively. They marched off to the back of the house together.

"When did *Kip* get here?"

"I can't keep track anymore. This place is nuts."

"Is the power out?"

"Yes. I'm not sure it's just us," Jen said from the front window. "Look, I don't see any lights on at the big house either."

A frantic knock on our door startled us all; I almost shrieked, and was glad of the dark. Jen hollered, "Who is it?"

"Bonfire time!" came JoJo's merry voice. "Everyone down to the beach!"

Jen snorted and opened the door. JoJo wasn't alone; was that Clary with him? Seemed like it. And who else? Whoever they were, even in the pitch black, it was clear that they were roaring drunk, snickering and nudging each other like five-year-olds. Or actors.

"You go on ahead and get started, JoJo; we'll be *right* behind you." Jen's tone was droll, amused.

"No way! We need help!" He put the back of his hand dramatically against his forehead, a pose rendered even more dramatic by being lit only by our little hearth fire. "We cannot POSSIBLY manage such a monumental undertaking on our own. You, fair and mighty maiden, must assist!" He reached for Jen—was he seriously trying to squeeze her bicep?—but missed as she stepped deftly back.

"Whoah, big boy," she said, reaching out for the bottle he held, probably to put it somewhere safe.

"Nope! Mine!" He raised the bottle high, sloshing amber-colored liquid around, spilling only a few drops. Then he leered at her. "Though if you're real nice to me, I might share."

And then I heard the telltale rumble of Kevin's big-ass RV working its way down the driveway again. "No, no, no!" I said. "Fine—let's go make the biggest damn bonfire in the history of bonfires and throw my stupid ex-boyfriend on it!" I stomped over to JoJo. "I'm in. What's in that bottle?"

The bright beam of the police flashlight heralded Kip and my dad's return from their investigations. "Nope, fuses all fine," Kip said. "I think it's—"

"It's an island-wide power outage!" JoJo cried. "And rather than curse the darkness, we're building a magnificent bonfire on the beach! Family tradition! Come one, come all!" He grabbed my arm—the uninjured one, thank goodness—and led the still-giggling Clary and the other woman (gorgeous, Asian, and I couldn't discern anything further in the dark) on a march across my pitch-black lawn.

"You might want some light—" Kip started.

"Come on then!" I hollered over my shoulder. "Before this fool kills us all!"

❦

I was certainly glad that the Brixton "kids" were behind this bonfire idea, because if my family and friends had created a gigantic pile of driftwood on her private stretch of beach, Diana would have fired me on the spot.

The woodpile was in the process of being gathered by a ragged and unruly crowd. Me, my parents, Cliff, Jen, Kip, Colin—and, of course, Kevin. All the campgrounds were closed for the season, and with the power out, even the ferries were scrambling to function. (I tried not to think about how suspiciously quickly he'd shown up here after the power went out; we were at least a twenty-minute drive from the ferry landing, in a normal car.) He swore he'd leave tomorrow, on the same ferry that my folks were leaving on, midday, and would not bring up the ridiculous "reality TV show" idea again.

Or the proposal.

JoJo and Clary and Maxine—the other woman turned out to be Clary's girlfriend—were less effective at gathering wood, but they were certainly entertaining, since they were all so drunk they could barely stand. Clary and Maxine were both so beautiful and arch, they seemed more like sisters than lovers, even though Maxine was Chinese.

We'd only been gathering wood for a few minutes when Lisa's troupe had joined us again; six (now they were six, somehow) loudmouthed, dramatic clowns dragging logs here and there, making jokes about hiding bodies, maenads and bacchanals, and the Salem witch trials. They seemed really fun, but I had some trouble remembering who was who. And they still, despite their antics, seemed kind of a closed set. I'd have to get to know them better if they were going to do my play—my play, which I hadn't *touched* since all these people descended on my house.

I was missing my solitude like crazy.

I had to look away from the growing pile, because it made me shiver. Even with all the hilarity around me, my mind kept wandering back to my experience of a week before, when I'd found Megan's body in a driftwood tangle.

Looking away took my eyes to the boat moored at Lisa's dock. The boat I'd agreed to sneak onto later tonight.

And where was Lisa? Home alone in her dark, plundered house? I peered up the beach, but of course could see nothing through the trees and darkness.

It couldn't have been much later than five o'clock, but at this time of year, full dark came early. JoJo splashed our pile of driftwood with his bottle and lit it on fire, flames whooshing up, scenting the air with the perfume of expensive brandy.

"I see a problem," he groused after a minute. "We stacked so much wood that we didn't leave anywhere to sit."

"So get some more logs," said Clary, rolling her eyes. "There's more washing up over there, go get one of those!"

"Those will be wet and heavy."

Maxine punched him in the shoulder. "Let's carry some up here. The fire will dry it out in no time, and you'll have somewhere to sit, you big sissy."

"Sissy?" He laughed out loud. "No one's ever called me a *sissy* before. Come help me with this log, I'll show you who's a sissy."

They staggered down the beach, Clary trailing after. In their state, I didn't think they should be near the water at all, but I certainly wasn't going to argue with them. I was perfectly happy to stand between my parents, feeling safe and enjoying the flames, how they danced, shooting sparks up into the stars. Skies were so dark here, and I loved it. I knew these same stars were in Seattle's night skies, but I had never seen them. They were hiding in all the light pollution.

I took some covert looks at the people standing around the fire.

Kevin looked, I had to admit, somewhat adorable. He was holding forth on the virtues of homemade marshmallows to

Jen. She looked interested, but she was probably more amused than anything else. Because, really? Homemade marshmallows? My brother was on her other side, joining in now and then. Kip stood just a bit apart from everyone else, holding his hands out to the flames to warm them. He hadn't had a sip of alcohol, and his civilian duds were just as pressed and tidy as his uniform, but I thought by his pleasant smile that he might be enjoying himself. He was so buttoned-up that it was hard to tell, but I decided to believe that he was.

And then, Colin. Scruffy and strong and sweet. Colin just kept showing up.

"Kip?" It was JoJo, suddenly sober, his arms around a shivering Clary. "Kip. We've found something." He thrust his sister at me. "Can you take care of Clary?"

She threw off his arm, shivering visibly. "I'm *fine*. No one needs to take *care* of me."

"Where's Maxine?"

"She's back down the beach. She's waiting with the…with the body."

CHAPTER 9

I didn't gasp or vanish or anything.

And yet three men rushed, not down the beach, but to me. Colin, Kevin and Kip, rushing to my side with concerned and gallant faces, all three of them slightly fluffed up with concern and care, like peacocks.

Oh, for god's sake, I'd just about had it.

The old me would have been afraid, in danger of disappearing, but I'd had a beer or three, plus the glass of wine earlier at Lisa's, and maybe even a swig of JoJo's fine brandy; but much more than that, I was too angry at all of them to vanish. Colin looked like he wanted to cry. Kevin had hold of my arm just above the elbow, holding firmly, pinching a little—something he *knew* annoyed me. "Are you...okay, Cam? You're not going to faint or anything, are you?"

"Of course I'm not going to faint. Why would I faint? Have you ever seen me faint, Kevin?" I yanked my arm away. "If there's a dead body to tend to, why are you all staring at *me*?"

Kip took a step back as Jen moved toward me. "Well, with the recent events, you can hardly blame the man for being concerned," Kip said. "Or, er, any of us, for that matter."

Oh my gosh, what was this? Were they all *friends*, now? Was Kip *scolding* me?

Kip drew himself up, looking taller than his modest height

would seem to allow. "Have you forgotten that you were kidnapped and shot this last week? Concern for you is only natural."

"SHOT?" My mother sounded like she was going to faint.
"Kidnapped and *shot?* Shot WHERE? Why didn't you TELL us?"

Well, that cat was out of the bag. And there was no getting it
back in. "Mom, it was just a graze. Only a few stitches, I swear."

"Camille! You are *not* staying here!"

"We knew you'd been kidnapped. But you could have found
a time to tell us that you were *shot*, Cam, sometime before two
outs in the bottom of the ninth!" My father sounded like he was
going to puke.

Jen, now standing just beside me, put her hand on my arm.
Unlike the men's attention, this felt comforting; I welcomed her
stabilizing presence. "There hasn't been a good time," I told my
parents. "I've been overwhelmed with all this company."

"There was nothing in the paper about you being *shot*," said
Kevin.

Cliff shook his head. "You can't stay here."

It wasn't my intention to treat the people who cared about me
with anger, but this just made me furious. "The authorities didn't
let everything get to the newspapers," I snapped. *Active investigation* and all that. "And if you're all that *concerned* about me, then
why don't we find out who is *behind* all this."

"She has a point." JoJo, the voice of reason, though the voice
was shaky right now. I looked up to see his face, drawn and som-
ber in the reflection of the flames. Finding dead bodies was the
only thing that could shake his composure, I decided.

And JoJo Brixton had found two in three days. Massacre Bay
was really living up to its name. But speaking of dead bodies!
"Kip, don't you need to—I don't know—go *look* at the body
maybe?"

"Right!" said Jen; her fingers clutched my arm a little harder.
And now her eyes were shining. Jen was *excited*.

The deputy sheriff shook himself a little before giving me a rueful glance, the firelight on his face accentuating his discomfort. "Yes. I just…I guess I was just enjoying the last few moments where any of this was my investigation." Then he shrugged his fine shoulders, turned to JoJo, and said, "All right, you'd better show me."

JoJo waved in the general direction of Lisa's beach. "Down there. You can't miss it. Maxine's standing by it. Don't make me go down there and look at it again." It was too dark to see if his face was green, but his voice made it pretty clear. I took a small step farther away from him. I didn't need barf on my shoes, on top of everything else.

Kip took off without another word. I could tell Jen was dying to follow him, but her loyalty to me won out. Barely.

The fire crackled. JoJo sat down, hard, on the ground. "Oh for crying out loud," Clary said. "Let's take care of *you*, you big sissy." She reached down for her brother's hand; he allowed himself to be pulled back to his feet.

"I need a drink," he muttered as she started to walk him back up to the big house.

Seemed like that was the last thing anyone needed, JoJo particularly, but none of us said so.

"I want to go up to the house and turn all the lights on," I said with a shiver. "But I don't want to leave this fire."

"And anyway, it wouldn't do any good," Kevin pointed out, helpfully.

"I want to know more about your getting *shot*!" my mom said, coming up to me and pulling me away from Jen to draw me into her own arms.

I shook my head, though I was grateful for her concern. "I don't want to talk about it now, not out here. I'll tell you everything…later. When the lights come back on."

Dad looked up the hill into the utter darkness. "Do you get power outages often here on the island?"

I shrugged. "I don't know. This is my first one." Well, the first one not caused by nefariousness, anyway.

That I knew of.

"We can go to the Intruder," Kevin offered.

"*What?*" I gaped at him.

"It has battery power—I can run the interior lights for hours, and if they run down, I can drive around a little and charge them up."

"Oh, your RV, right. Jeez. I can't believe that's really its name. Who thought that was a good idea?"

Kevin grinned. "I dunno. It's what the manufacturer named this model. I think it's funny. Ironic."

Of course you do, you freakin' hipster. That's obviously why you rented it. Bought it. Whatever. "No, let's stay by the fire."

My mom pulled me into another fierce hug. Clearly not wanting to let me go. "Are you truly okay, Camille? Where were you shot?"

Behind us, Dad added, "Tell us everything. Please."

They weren't going to let this go, were they? I sighed, glancing at Cliff, who nodded. Then Jen said, "I can tell them the story. You just relax."

"There still aren't any logs to sit on," I pointed out.

 ✎

Colin and Jen managed to procure a few plastic chairs from somewhere—the Brixtons' garden shed, maybe. They were a little dusty, but much better than sitting on the cold, damp shingle of a beach. And then, between the two of us, Jen and I told my parents, and Cliff and Kevin, the whole story.

Somewhere in all the commotion of earlier, Lisa's troupe of actors had vanished again. Were they even individual people, or did they only move in a pack? Anyway, I was glad they were gone. It made telling the story easier.

"Oh, Cam," my mom said, after Jen had described the rescue—she and Colin and Kip saving me from the seriously disturbed Sheila. "And her body was never found? Do you think that's who's…" She waved helplessly down the beach.

"I don't want to say I hope so, exactly, but…"

"*I* hope so," Jen put in. "We'll all sleep a lot easier knowing she's not out there looking for revenge or something."

"You're not helping!" I said.

The crunch of footsteps on the beach startled us all; the sight of Kip's monster flashlight was a relief.

"Who is it?" I sprang to my feet and rushed over to the deputy. "Who's dead?"

"Well, now, you know I can't—"

"Don't do that," I interrupted. "If it's not even going to be your investigation anymore, can you at least tell me whether it was Sheila?"

Kip gave me a strange look. "How did you know it was a woman?"

Fear stabbed me in the gut; my heart raced. "I didn't. I just… come on, Kip, was it Sheila?"

He shook his head and glanced at Jen, who had come to stand right at my elbow again. "You ladies will be the end of me. The deceased did not appear to be Sheila Bukowski, though the coroner will have to confirm any identity."

"Have you called for backup?" Jen asked.

Kip glared at her. "And who appointed *you* San Juan County Sheriff? Of course I called; the boat will be here any minute." At his belt, his radio gave a staticky burst of unintelligible gabble; he reached down and slid the volume knob lower. "Now, if you all will excuse me, I have actual law enforcement business to attend to." He stalked off into the dark, toward the guesthouse.

"Touchy much?" Jen asked as she led me back to the bonfire. "He didn't tell us anything," she added, to the group gathered there.

"Oh, one more thing," Kip added, stepping back into the light from the bonfire. "I'm going to need everybody to stay on the premises here."

"What?" Jen asked, disbelief strong in her voice.

Kip's mouth tightened; he wasn't happy about it either. "Not my doing. It's the word from above. No one leaves until the proper inquiries are accomplished. We will need to question everyone." He gave us all what he probably supposed was a stern, cop-like glare, and left again.

"Not every day we get the sheriff over here," Colin remarked. "That Sheila just continues to be trouble."

"It's definitely not Sheila," came a voice from the dark behind us.

"Oh crap, Maxine, you almost gave me a heart attack," Jen said, as Clary's girlfriend joined us. "Tell us everything."

I marveled yet again at Jen, at the way she so comfortably became familiar with everyone—and they with her. Years of bartending and waiting tables, I supposed; plus her own natural charm.

Maxine was surprisingly matter-of-fact. "It's a middle-aged woman, but I know it's not that Sheila character. Your country cop talks a good game, but when push comes to shove, he's crap at managing information." She settled herself right up to the edge of the bonfire. "He made his whole radio call in to headquarters with me standing right there, like he'd forgotten all about me. And then he got another call, and went through it all again. I think this is a big deal."

"Wow," Jen said. "On our little island."

"So...what did she look like?" I asked Maxine.

"Caucasian. Tall, rangy. Middle-aged, like I said; maybe forty-five, fifty? I don't know. Brown hair. She'd been in the water for a while, but she had a wound on the back of the head. Probably from a fall—he thinks she must have slipped and hit her head, and fell in the water, either unconscious or already dead."

My stab of fear from earlier returned, harder this time. I sucked in a small breath.

"That's got to be the woman you saw on the boat!" Jen hissed, loud enough for everyone to hear.

"The boat?" my father asked, his voice gruff and disapproving. "What boat? Didn't that fellow's boat get impounded?"

"This is a different boat," I said, squirming and trying to get a handle on my fear. "This...um...well, this was the boat that belonged to Lisa Cannon's intruder. It's been at her dock since Wednesday."

"My goodness," my mom said. "And you saw someone on it? When?"

"Mom, I just saw..."

"We have to go *look*," Jen said, her voice insistent. "You have to *identify* her."

"What?" I gaped at her. "Kip told us to stay here."

"He told us to stay *on the premises*," Jen said. "The beach is the premises. We need to see if that's the woman you saw. It'll help with his case."

My dad shook his head. "I'm sure if the deputy wanted Camille to identify the body, he would have asked her to."

Jen turned to him. "But he doesn't know Cam saw her!"

"Jen!" I protested. "You're freaking my parents out. And he *does* know."

"Then he should have asked you to look! Just come look at the body!"

I looked at my parents, and my brother. They looked stunned and frightened, and, well, who could blame them? "This all just keeps...unfolding," Mom said. "What else you haven't told us?"

My cheeks burned. "Um, that's pretty much it." *Pretty much.* Except for Lisa's binder, which I needed to get off that boat before it was swarmed with cops. Oh crap, had I really agreed to do that? Why me?

"Are you sure it's safe to live out here, so far from civilization?"

"Mom—" I started, but yet again, dear Jen came to my rescue. "Actually, we have *so* much less crime than the big city," she said. "Have you checked Seattle's homicide rates lately?"

"Hey," said Maxine, "speaking of homicide, did Clary head up to the house?"

I gaped at her. What did *that* mean? She just grinned saucily back at me.

"Yeah," Jen said. "With JoJo. He wasn't doing so well, I don't think."

"City boy," Colin murmured, but without rancor.

I turned to look up the hill. Still dark everywhere: guesthouse, Brixton house, Lisa's estate. And so quiet, so very quiet.

Maxine got up. "I guess I'll go find them. Anyone got a flashlight?"

"Kip took his," I said, glancing around the firepit. Everyone shook their heads.

"That's all right," Maxine said. "Don't worry about me at all, wandering through the dark scary woods all alone late at night. As long as I'm not prowling around on a boat where I don't belong, I'm sure I'll be fine."

"What?" I gasped. "Do you think—whoever did it—are they still—"

Maxine laughed, obviously thinking I was joking. "'Did it'? Nobody 'did it'. Didn't you hear me? Your country cop thinks she slipped, hit her head and fell into the water." She shrugged. "I'll be fine: no water to fall in up here. Though if you hear a crash, come find me." She sauntered up the hillside.

"Come on," Jen said, getting up and dragging me to my feet as soon as Maxine was gone. "We need to go get a look at the body, quick, before the reinforcements arrive and get in the way." A light sparked in her hand.

"Wait, you've got a flashlight?"

She snickered and aimed the device toward me. "It's my *phone*, silly. I wasn't going to give Maxine my *phone*."

"You're not going to go *down* there, are you?" my mom asked, her voice tremulous.

And then Colin was beside us. "I'll go with them. Ms. Darling won't give this a rest till we do, Mrs. Tate. I'll protect them, and we'll be right back."

My dad, Cliff, and Kevin all stared back at us. I could almost see their brains whirring, trying to decide if they should insist on coming too—or on staying here to "protect" my mother.

Colin was right. Jen wasn't going to let us *not* go, so we might as well do it. "We'll be fine," I told my folks. "Don't worry about us."

"Little late for that," my dad grumbled.

Jen tugged on my arm again. "Come on, come on."

As ever, I felt like she enjoyed all this intrigue just a little too darn much.

She shone her phone light on the ground before us. Colin walked on the other side of me as we made our way down the rocky shingle. To the unmarked dividing line between the Brixton beach and Lisa's; past Snooks's boat, police-taped off; past the other side of Lisa's little dock; then down another short stretch of beach…and there it was.

"Ugh," Jen said, playing the light over the body. "Yep, that's pretty dead."

Colin's hand tightened on my arm, and when exactly had he taken my arm? But I didn't pull away. I stood there and stared down at a bare shoulder, a tangle of salt-crusted hair that threaded and tangled around a pile of rocks. I forced myself to look for the particulars, to see what, if anything, I could recognize. Could identify. I remembered a baseball cap and a ponytail and bright, sharp eyes. But the hat was gone, along with whatever else she'd been wearing when she went into the water. It was like the ocean had taken away her clothing, and dressed her in seaweed and storm wrack.

"Are you okay?" Jen sounded concerned. I nodded, and she held her phone's flashlight steady on the woman's face. Her eyes were empty and open, washed to paleness by death and seawater.

But yes. Middle-aged, and about the right build, and the hair was dark. All wet hair is dark, a funny fact that hairdressers know, but this could have been the same color I'd seen in the starlight. "I guess this could be her," I said, then swallowed. Does death do this to people, wash away their individuality and make them all the same?

Or maybe it was just bodies in the water, washed ashore.

I was shivering, remembering Megan's body. At least I'd had so much to drink today, I was apparently in no danger of disappearing. And at least, this time, I wasn't alone.

"All right," Colin said. "That's enough. Let's get on back to the others."

We walked in silence back to the bonfire. Even Jen had stopped chirping.

My folks, my brother, and Kevin sat in silence around the bonfire. "Well?" Cliff asked.

"It's probably her," I told them all. "I think. I only saw her in the dark."

"On that boat after the break-in?" my dad asked. "When?"

"Um, just the other day," I said, trying to sound casual. "From a distance. I was passing by, um, going to see Lisa, and I noticed movement. But I didn't get a super close look or anything."

"I still think you should tell the deputy what you saw," my mom put in.

I nodded vigorously. "I already did, Mom. I told him the day after Thanksgiving, the morning after I saw her."

"But you didn't tell *us*?"

"I didn't want to alarm everyone." *Please, everyone, just drop this.*

"No more questions." Colin got up. "Guess the entire county's worth of law enforcement isn't rushing over here after all." He dragged another log onto the fire. Sparks shot up into the sky, flickering out into the dark night.

"Do you think Kip really thinks it was an accident?" I was asking Jen, but Colin answered.

"Seems if he thought we were in danger, he wouldn't let us sit down here on the beach."

He had a point.

"He didn't even tell us not to go look at her," Jen said, a little defensively. As if already working up her argument for Kip, when he learned that we had.

I tried to remember exactly what he'd said. "I thought he said we should stay here," I said, waving at the bonfire.

"Whatever." Jen shrugged. "Anyway," she added, "who thinks dumping bodies in the water is a good idea? They always wash back up."

"Like all those feet that wash ashore over on Vancouver," Colin put in.

Despite the roaring fire, I shivered again in the dark.

⁊

We were tired and cold, and law enforcement had finally arrived. "Stay where I can find you," Kip warned us all. "We'll have questions."

Well, I had questions too. Lots of questions. And one tiny, possible answer. "Kip," I said, hanging back as the rest of the crowd climbed the hill to the still-dark houses above.

He paused, clearly wanting to follow the other uniforms. "What is it, Ms. Tate?"

"I need to tell you that Jen and Colin and I went to look at the body, after you left us down here," I blurted out in a breathless rush. "I know you didn't say we should, but—um—Jen thought we should see if I recognized her. The woman. The body."

"And did you?"

"Maybe. I think so. I think she could have been the woman I saw on the boat."

He gazed at me another moment, then nodded. "Thank you for that." Then he turned away.

"Wait," I said, as he started to walk down the beach. "Is that all?"

"Of course not," he called over his shoulder. "But go home for now; we'll get to the questioning after we've secured the scene."

I walked up the hill and found Colin and Jen standing on the guesthouse porch. "Where's everyone else?" I asked them.

"Looking for candles," Jen said. "Where were you? I turned around and you were gone."

I held her gaze. "I wanted to tell Kip that we'd gone to look at her."

She just nodded.

"How long do you think he'll make us stay?" Colin asked. "Need to get back to my boat soon, make sure the battery back-up came on."

"Your guess is as good as mine," I said.

"This is so dumb," Jen said. "You told him what we saw; we don't know what happened to her. I need to get home too."

"At least there's plenty of food here," I said.

Jen smiled. "Yeah, but we shouldn't open your fridge till the power comes back on. Which could be a while."

I shivered. "It's about as cold as a fridge out here. We could just keep things out on the back porch."

"Well, that's true."

I glanced over at the main house. Candlelight flickered in a few windows on the third floor, but I heard nothing. "I wonder where Diana and Emmett are? Have they just been sitting in the dark this whole time?"

"If they were smart, they took off for Rosario the moment the lights went out," Jen said. "They have not only a big-ass generator but their own whole power plant. The rest of the island goes dark, and Rosario still serves gourmet dinners cooked in a real kitchen. And their spa has hot showers."

"Seriously?" I needed to check this place out. "Good to know." I wondered if Lisa had gone there too. "Smart of them to be gone when all the drama came down."

"Indeed." I watched the candlelight in JoJo's bedroom window for another moment, then peered down toward the beach. The sheriff's boat had docked at the community pier, and two more official Washington State vehicles had arrived up here, parked next to Kip's truck (though neither of them was marked "coroner") and blocking us all in—finishing the job the Intruder had started. Down the hill, I could see occasional spots of light, probably flashlights moving around, but couldn't really tell what was going on. If anything. And recent experience had told me that, whatever they did or didn't do about the body, it would take a while. "Well, should we head inside?" I asked.

"Sure," Colin said.

"No place else to go, I guess," Jen added.

Kevin was building up the fire in the fireplace, and doing a piss-poor job of it, even I could tell that. "Shove over, let me do that," I said.

He gave me a helpless grin. "Sorry. I guess it's more complicated than it looks."

"Not really. Smaller pieces on the bottom, bigger pieces up top. And leave it enough air, you're smothering it." Not that that was a metaphor for anything. Anyway, I felt proud, competent all out of proportion to what it merited, when I got the fire blazing and snapping a minute later.

Cliff came in, holding a lit birthday candle. "Mealy, you are seriously under-equipped here."

"Where did you even find that?" I hadn't ever bought birthday candles.

He grinned, spooky in the firelight. "Little cabinet above the stove."

"Ah. I can't reach that cabinet."

My folks followed him in from the kitchen, both empty-handed. "So, what now?" my dad asked as my mom yawned.

"We wait for the cops to come talk to us, I guess," I said.

"I'm ready to go to bed," my mom said. "How long do you think they'll take down there?"

"I don't know. What time is it?" I pulled out my cell phone: nearly eight-thirty. "Huh, it feels both later and earlier than that."

"It's been a long day," my mom said. "And we've got lots of digesting to do still. I think I'm going to turn in. You can wake me up when it's time to testify."

"Okay." She was right; and it had been an even longer day for me than anyone knew. And it wasn't over yet...probably. In a way, I was relieved that there were cops all over the beach and the boat. Was I off the hook for Lisa's search?

But no. This just made it all that much more urgent. What if they impounded the boat, sailed or tugged it away? What if *they* found Lisa's documents?

Before my brain weasels could go further, I realized Mom had a good point. I wasn't sleepy, but I was feeling overwhelmed, and my tiny, dark house was filled with people, several of whom were clearly wishing they could go home now. Except we'd all been ordered to stay here. I could at least escape into my bedroom and close the door. I yawned too, trying to be convincing. "Hey, can you guys wake me up too? I'm just wiped."

"Sure thing," Jen said.

"Thanks." I gave her a hug, waved goodnight to everyone, and closed myself in my bedroom. "James?" I whispered into the darkness, but he didn't answer. I fumbled with my phone, lighting my way to the bed. I wished I could lie here and read, but oh well. Just a little alone time, down time, should do me a world of good.

But I had a plan. This night wasn't over for me, not at all.

I set my phone's alarm for one a.m., and closed my eyes.

CHAPTER 10

I woke up after I didn't know how long. It was pitch-black, the power still out, judging by the fact that my bedside clock wasn't flashing 12:00, 12:00, 12:00. I stared at the ceiling a minute, wondering which lights had been left on in the house. It was going to startle the hell out of us all when the power came back on at three a.m.

When I got up to go look at that boat, I could check the switches.

Unless the boat had already been impounded? God, I hoped not.

I had to decide if I was really going to do it. Because that woman's death might have been accidental, or it might not. I had no idea. If someone killed her, and she'd been on that boat, would someone do the same to me?

But I had a tool that stranger never had at her disposal. I could vanish, I reminded myself. My curse could be my gift, if I were really in danger again.

I was so tired of running and hiding and vanishing. I was ready to be brave.

I got up and pulled my robe on, then flicked my curtains aside so I could see the driveway. No sheriff cars. I hadn't even heard them leave, I'd been that zonked out.

Had they already questioned everyone? And they didn't want

to talk to me? Okay, this was too weird. Or maybe Kip was protecting me, yet again. I mean, he knew I hadn't been anywhere near the body, but still, this was annoying. I was getting really, really tired of being treated like a child, or a delicate feminine flower.

My cell phone informed me that it was now twelve forty-five, that it had no service, and that its battery was at 17 percent. I canceled the one a.m. alarm, then switched the phone off, powering it all the way down.

I had to just put my clothes on, go down, and search that boat. Without a flashlight, even?

No, of course not. There had to be a flashlight somewhere. If it was true that this island lost power regularly, the Brixtons would surely have a stash of emergency supplies.

The Brixtons—right. I pulled the curtains aside again and looked over at the main house. No lights in the windows, not even candles. Maybe Emmett and Diana were still at Rosario, if that's where they'd gone. It was a resort, they could have gotten a room for the night. Maybe they hadn't been allowed back on the estate; maybe the whole place was sealed off. I wished somebody had let me know what was going on.

I sighed again, letting the curtain drop and the darkness enfold me once more. "Come on, Cam," I whispered, feeling around for my jeans.

If I had a flashlight here, my family would have already found it in their hunt for candles. So, to the main house it was.

Even with two sweaters on, it was uncomfortably brisk outside. I hurried across the drive and around to the front of the big house.

Dark, quiet. No signs of life whatsoever. I stood at the ostentatious front door, second-guessing myself. Should I knock? Should I just let it go, go back to bed? Surely Lisa would understand…

"You can't sleep either?"

I whirled around, gasping. My upper arms flared up into full tingle. I could just barely see a long lean dark shape, angled against his Jaguar; my breath sighed back out of me.

"Crap, JoJo, you scared the dickens out of me."

He giggled. "'Dickens'? Really, Cam?" I heard the low sound of him sipping something, then the clunk of a glass set onto the car's hood. "As a writer, you have to be able to do better than that."

I made my way over to the car, hoping there weren't any rocks or things in my path. Once there, I leaned next to him. "No, I can't sleep. What's that you've got there?"

"Well, *somebody* finished all the brandy, so I had to open a bottle of Mom's Frangelico. It's nasty. Want some?"

"Yes." I put my hand out; a glass found its way there. I took a tentative sip. "Well. I suppose I've had worse."

He chuckled softly.

"You shouldn't have poured all your brandy on the bonfire," I added.

"Oh, is that what happened." He took the glass back and sipped. "Silly me. What the *dickens* was I thinking?"

"Very funny."

We stood there in the dark and cold for a minute. He offered the sweet, syrupy stuff again, and I took another sip.

"So, you want to talk about it?" he asked.

"About what?"

Beside me, I could feel him gesture—a shrug, perhaps. "Oh, I don't know. Anything. Ex-boyfriends. Dead bodies. You know."

"I just came over to see if you guys had a flashlight I could borrow."

"Uh-huh."

I reached out for the glass again. It was getting low. "Was that 'uh-huh' you have a flashlight or 'uh-huh' you don't believe me?"

JoJo chuckled again. "Both, I guess. But yes, we have several flashlights." He didn't move.

"I don't know what to think about any of it. The ex-boyfriends or the dead bodies or, well, any of it," I said, after another minute.

"That seems fair."

"I know that coming here, to the island I mean, I was running away," I said. "I knew it at the time, and I know it now. It's what I do. But you can't run away from yourself."

"Now *that's* profound." He offered the glass again. "Drink more; maybe you can come up with more Zen koans." But he said it kindly, almost without mockery.

"So why can't *you* sleep?" Fair was fair: if he could interrogate me, I could turn the tables on him. "Did Kip and his gang question you all?"

"No, they knocked on the door about midnight and said they'd be back to talk to everyone in the morning. And that we should all continue not leaving the premises."

"Ah." Well, that was okay then. I silently forgave Kip. This time.

JoJo waved vaguely toward the house; my eyes were adjusting, I could just barely see it. "I couldn't sleep with the sound of all that shrieking lesbian sex in there."

"*Really?*"

He laughed. "No. I just wanted to see if I could shock you. Clary and Maxine are very considerate."

"Um. Well. Good." I stared off into the darkness. The nutty liqueur seemed to coat my mouth, my throat, though it burned pleasantly in my stomach. And, of course, my chameleoning had settled entirely back down. Should I have some more? Just how much *had* I drunk today? Yesterday; whatever.

"Imagine, a simple slip—one tiny wrong step—that can end it all," he said, after another long pause. "Hit your head, fall into the water: boom, all over. Everything you are, every thought in your head, all the potential of your life, just gone. Your body now just a piece of meat, decaying in the water."

"All right, hand it over," I said, reaching for the glass. He did; I took a big swallow, and he followed suit when I handed it back.

"How many times a day do we trip or slip or stumble?" he went on. "How many moments of inattention? We glance away when driving. We don't turn the gas stove off all the way."

"We rob some nice lady's house and keel over from a heart attack," I put in.

"Hm. That too."

"Well," I said, after another few minutes had passed. I was really starting to shiver now, despite the two sweaters and the too-much, too-sweet liquor curdling in my belly.

JoJo turned to face me, though I could still barely see him. "I guess you want that flashlight now."

"Please."

He led me into the grand, dark house and down the long hallway toward the kitchen. JoJo clearly knew the house by rote; I followed his soft footsteps, trusting him not to run me into anything. It's amazing how dark a house can be, without all the little lights you don't even consciously notice: the microwave clock, the TV, all the various chargers and appliances and indicator lights.

I remembered my first night here, my first night on the island: this house had looked so bright, this kitchen so sleek and gleaming. And large and empty. Now—

"Cover your eyes," JoJo warned.

I did, and heard a click.

"Okay, you can look, but be careful."

I spread my fingers, letting in the absolutely blinding beam of a flashlight. He had thoughtfully aimed it across the room, but still I could feel my pupils shrink in alarm. I blinked a few times. "I'm not sure I've ever lived anywhere so dark."

"It takes some getting used to," he said. "But then you do. Now that I've moved to Seattle, I have a hard time sleeping at night. Sometimes I wonder if I made the right decision."

You could move back, I wanted to say, but stopped myself. The reason I had this job at all was because JoJo wasn't living in this huge house anymore. As much as I was growing to like him, there was no possible scenario in which we were cool, cozy sitcom next-door neighbors. "Why did you move away?" I asked, instead.

He gave that languorous chuckle again. "That's a longer story than I'm up for telling in the middle of the night. Or than you're probably up for listening to."

"Ah." Well, *now* I was all intrigued.

"But the short version is, I needed a change."

"Isn't that kind of always the reason for moving?"

He shrugged, handing me a second flashlight. "Here, this should get you through the night, anyway. I've kept them with fresh batteries."

"Thanks."

"Sleep well." He walked me back to the front door, then closed the door behind me. It felt weird not to give him a hug or something, but we weren't *that* close yet.

I walked back around the house, slowly. It was so late. Was I really going to prowl around that boat? Or was I just going back to bed? Dither, dither.

After everything that had already gone down, I really didn't want to do this. But I'd promised Lisa. Lisa who now trusted me, really *trusted* me. I didn't want to lose that.

And the woman was dead, right? And it was probably an accident. So there was no danger.

Right?

Unless it hadn't been an accident at all.

I stood next to the Intruder parked in front of the guesthouse, my flashlight pointing at the ground, mired in indecision.

Could I do this? I had to do this. Could I?

I knew I was tougher than I looked, tougher than even I usually believed I was. No one could have gone through the things I'd been through and not be tough, but it was more than just the trauma of what I'd witnessed, what I'd been subjected to. I remembered, in my earliest years, screaming red-faced and stomping my feet. I remembered hitting out with my fists, gnashing my teeth, even. Maybe I was just remembering two-year-old tantrums. I'd witnessed enough of those in the salon, along with embarrassed mothers assuring me that the child would "grow out of it."

Had I grown out of it? I didn't think so. Something had started to scare me, and I'd stopped being angry and lashing out. At some point, life became so terrifying that the safest thing to do was to disappear, to slip into a state of not being noticed. And that had overtaken me. It had grown to control my life. I had warnings before it happened. I could stave it off by having a drink or two, but I was terrified of leaning on that too heavily and having an entirely different problem to deal with.

The paralysis was the most frightening part. Aside from having a drink, nothing could prevent it—or make it happen. Until that day when Sheila had me confined. Then, for the first time in my life, I'd used it on purpose.

I had taken charge, taken control. Yes, I'd still gotten shot, and I'd had to be rescued; but in the crucial moment, I had saved myself. I had taken back possession of myself. That same possession that had been at the core of the screaming, thwarted two-year-old; only now, as an adult, I could act. I could decide.

I could decide who I wanted in my life, and who I didn't. And I could act to make it so.

I wanted to be the kind of person Lisa Cannon wanted to be friends with. I wanted to be who she already saw in me, who she believed me to be—and who she believed I could be.

I did *not* want to be the quiet, vanishing helpmeet girlfriend who would follow her dynamic, creative man around on his stupid quest to turn a giant RV into a food truck (and himself into a star) on reality television. I snorted quietly, glancing up again at the Intruder before turning and walking resolutely down the hill to the beach.

Snooks's boat was still there, the all-too-familiar "do not cross" yellow police tape flapping. There wasn't any additional tape; it didn't look like the authorities had done anything with it yet. All tonight's activities had been focused further down the beach, apparently.

Good. I had a chance.

I didn't even slow down.

Before I could talk myself out of it, I tucked the flashlight into the crook of my arm, careful to keep its beam low, and stepped over onto the vessel itself. It rocked gently under my weight. Unseen things creaked and clanked. I paused there, listening to be sure it was just chains and equipment I was hearing. It took a minute to satisfy myself that the boat wasn't going to sink under me. It was junky and cluttered, but seemed in surprisingly good shape otherwise. Weirdly, there were comfy places to sit out on the deck: long cushions on the side benches, and even an embroidered rocking chair. Then I remembered that Snooks made what living he had by ferrying folks over to Crane Island. Okay, so I guessed that made sense.

I thought about the dead woman. *Where* had she hit her head, exactly? On this boat? Or had she washed ashore from somewhere else?

Odd coincidence, if she'd come from farther afield.

But what had she been doing back on the boat?

I shook my head and told myself to get down to business, stop spooking myself. I took another step but stopped in my tracks once more. Did I hear a voice, a distant voice? I strained my ears, and tried to shut down my imagination. *Just listen, just listen.* I heard the creak again of something near the front of the boat, and the lapping of gentle waves against the posts of the dock and the sides of the boat. But nothing else.

I lifted the flashlight just a few inches, playing it across the deck on which I stood. Then I quickly covered the light with my hand and glanced upward, even though I knew I wouldn't be able to see any houses from here, the curve of the hill prevented it.

But even so, would anyone up there see the light down here? Maybe, just maybe they could. If they were also awake in the middle of the night, and staring down toward the water. In any event, I had to be more careful.

I opened my fingers just a hair, letting the light leak out only enough to let me find my way to the boat's tiny chicken-coop cabin. If Lisa's documents were on here somewhere, they were far more likely to be inside than out on the deck anyway. And I could hunt in there more easily without my light shining all over creation.

The cabin's door was unlocked—indeed, it didn't look as though it could lock. That was a relief. I let myself inside and pulled the heavy, bleached-wood door shut behind me.

It wasn't a whole lot warmer in here, but at least the walls and door kept the cold breeze out. I played the beam of the light around the small space. Wheel and controls for operating the boat; built-in shelves and cabinets; even more of the same kind of junk that I'd seen out on the deck. Where in the world did Snooks sleep? But tiny as the cabin was, it was so cluttered that it would take forever to hunt through here, even for something that hadn't been deliberately hidden. And the place had already clearly been searched, by at least Ms. Dead Woman, if not the cops. Even an untidy seaman wouldn't have left his boat like this; I could hardly find a bare patch of floor to step on.

So think, Cam, I said to myself. If one or two or ten people had already been through here, professional people, then either Lisa's binder had already been found and stolen or impounded or rehidden somewhere far away, or it was still here.

I had to go with "still here", or what was the point of my even doing this?

So. Where might a plain grey one-inch binder be, that people far cleverer than me (or at least people who were far more familiar with the ins and outs of boats) would have missed?

I stood in the center of the tiny cabin and closed my eyes, trying to visualize, trying to think. Ephraim Snooks was disturbed,
possibly crazy; but he had also been functional. He'd earned a
living, such as it was. He knew people and people knew him.

Why had he broken into Lisa's house and stolen such a peculiar
assortment of things? Drugs and underwear and a computer and
first aid supplies: okay, all stuff an unbalanced boat dude might
be drawn to.

But a binder full of important encryption materials, locked in
a hidden safe under her house? That was a whole different level
of theft. That was spy-novel stuff.

It was almost as if the other items were a smokescreen.

It was almost as if even Snooks himself—harmless well-known
local kook—was a smokescreen.

I leaned back against the pilot's chair, thinking through the
implications. The chair creaked and settled a little, so I didn't give
it all my weight.

Either Snooks was not what he seemed…or he hadn't been
acting alone.

Clearly he hadn't been acting undetected, or Ms. Dead Woman wouldn't have been prowling around on his boat. Looking for
something, and not finding it. Returning to look for it again…
and dying in the process.

Perhaps it was cold of me, but my next thought was, *God, I
hope she didn't find it and drop it into the water when she fell in.*

No. I had to proceed from the assumption that it was still here
on the boat. I'd never find anything in the water at night; probably wouldn't even in the daylight, even if I dared to look then,
which I didn't. Not with crime scene tape all over the place, and
a house full of family and friends and ex-boyfriends.

The binder was either here on the boat, and therefore I'd find
it; or it was not, and I would not.

If someone had put Snooks up to the whole thing, hoping to
disguise a very specific theft in the confusion of an inept bum-

bling robbery—but wait. Snooks was still in Lisa's house, clutching a bag of random weird loot, when he died. Yet Lisa told me she thought the binder was on this boat.

Unless Snooks came in, stole the binder, hid it on his boat, and then went back into the house to ransack it, do a little underwear-thieving, and fall over dead, then someone else must have taken the binder.

And hidden it here?

I wished I could talk to Lisa, but it was deep in the night, and I wasn't even sure she was home. I wished I'd asked her more questions at the time. First and foremost: *why* did she think the binder was here? She had seemed so confident about it, I hadn't thought to question her. But the more I considered it, the less it made sense.

I could just leave. Talk to Lisa in the morning. But I was here now; would I get another chance to sneak on board? No, I had to at least make a thorough search for it.

Leaving aside the larger questions of who might have stolen it, I thought about the possibility of someone who was not the owner of this boat hiding something here.

They'd have to know boats in general, and how they went together, and the places to stash things on them.

They'd have to know this boat, in its particulars and peculiarities.

They'd have to have had access to Snooks, to have somehow persuaded him to burgle Lisa's house at a particular time on a particular day. And they'd have to have been able to hide a binder here quickly, probably wanting to get it stashed and get gone in just a few minutes. (I was going to go with the assumption for now that they hadn't expected the man to drop dead on Lisa's fine white carpet.)

I sighed, leaning a little more heavily against the chair, feeling the weariness in my bones creep through me. I couldn't even sit on the chair, piled as it was with yet more clutter. The post mounting the chair into the floor (was it still a deck, inside the cabin?) creaked again as I gave it more of my weight, almost sounding like a little cry for help.

I straightened, then leaned again. The chair wobbled, not creaking this time.

Then I heard the cry.

I stepped back and shined the flashlight at the base of the chair. It was bolted to the floor with six screws…or at least, it should have been. Four of the screws were missing, and the fifth one was partly unscrewed. I bent down to look closer, and the cry resolved itself into a sound so familiar it made me gasp.

"James!" I hissed, rattling the heavy chair on its base.

"Meow!" he answered, from underneath the floorboards.

I scrambled to my feet, looking frantically around the trashed cabin for a screwdriver. Of course I couldn't find anything in the dark and the mess. "Meow!" James said again, clearly recognizing my voice.

"Hang in there!" I said. "I'm coming to save you!"

Where in the world…? *Forget it,* I thought, and went back to the chair, grabbing hold of it by its weathered arms and rattling it back and forth. It grew wobblier by the minute, as the second-to-last screw worked its way out. Soon I was able to lean over and unscrew it by hand.

"Meow!"

But that final screw held fast. It was a big, thick one, too; but the chair and its post were bigger and heavier. I flashed the light around the room a final time before giving the chair a hearty push.

It wrenched hard, pulling the last screw halfway out, splintering a floorboard in the process, then hit the floor with a heavy thunk. The boat rocked crazily; papers and items fluttered and fell all around me. I couldn't be bothered to figure out what they were.

"Meow!" An orange and white face poked through the gap in

the broken floorboard, far too small for even a scrawny-ass kitten like James to make his way through, but it was a good start.

"How did you even get *in* there?" I chided him, as I searched the room once more, this time looking for something to pry up more boards with. Where was a good hefty crowbar when you needed one?

And who *were* these wicked criminals? That focused, fierce woman; and, behind her somewhere, Lisa's ex-husband.

It was bad enough when they were trying to do damage to Lisa Cannon. But now they had tried to kill my cat.

This was war.

"Aha!" I found leaning in the corner behind the door, not a crowbar, but a long pole with a hook on the end. It was quite sturdy. I tried not to think about what such a thing would be useful for on a boat but simply deployed the hook-end into the frayed floorboard, after convincing my foolish cat to get out of the way.

Cats are not at all obedient, of course, but James had at least enough of a measure of self-preservation—and lack of panic—to withdraw just enough for me to get the pole down into the tiny space he was in. A few good wrenches, and five or six splintered floorboards came up. Thank god this was such an old, weathered boat. The wood should not have been that easy to pry loose.

Except of course it was, because I wasn't the first person to pry it up in the last few days. And whoever had done it had trapped my curious cat. James leapt out of the small space and prowled around the cabin, meowing and purring, quite pleased with himself. I petted him almost absently with one hand as my other hand reached in and pulled out the grey binder.

"Bingo."

"Meow!"

❧

With a flashlight and a binder tucked under one arm and a

squirmy cat under the other, I made my careful way back off the boat, mindful of not hitting my head and falling into the inky water below. Once we were safely on the dock, I put James down and shifted my burdens. I had glanced into the binder on the boat, just to be sure it was what I was looking for; lines of impenetrable code. This had to be it.

Once back on the beach, I contemplated shutting the flashlight off and waiting for my eyes to readjust so I could find my way home without leaking light all over the place, but then my weariness—and relief—hit me full force. If anyone caught me up and about at this weird hour, I had James with me. I had been looking for my cat all day, and now I had found him. No one should wonder further.

Turned out I didn't have to worry about it. I let James and myself in the back door of the guesthouse and checked around for light switches in the "up" position while James scarfed down the contents of his food bowl, then drank his water all the way down. Jen snored on the couch in the living room, by the dying embers of the fire; Colin must have joined Cliff and Kevin in the Intruder. I shook my head, thinking about all those unused guest rooms in the main house, but oh well.

Then I hid the binder between my mattress and box spring (taking a page from poor Megan Duquesne's book, as it were) and crawled into bed with my cat. At long, long last.

Someone had hidden this book under that floorboard recently. Who was it? And why would they put it there in the first place?

I was too tired to figure it out. And James was purring like a motor.

Saturday

CHAPTER 11

The good news was that the power came back on at six in the morning.

The bad news was that I had missed the switch on my bedside lamp; and, having been up half the night, I was actually, for once in my life, still sleeping at that late hour.

I jerked awake, confused and muzzy-headed. James barely stirred on the pillow beside me, curled into the crook of my neck, drooling on my shoulder.

"Hey! Lights!" came my dad's voice from out in the hall.

"So get some coffee started already," I heard Mom mutter to him.

I sat up and blinked, ran my hands through my hair, and smiled. I'd missed my folks. I was so glad they were here, and sorry they had to leave today…if they were going to be allowed to leave today, I remembered, fast on the heels of the first thought.

Right. Another crime scene, another mysterious investigation. When would the authorities be back to question us all? Soon, I was sure.

I got up and dug around in my dresser for clean jeans, T-shirt, and sweatshirt. James gave a little mew of protest when I removed my body heat from the bed, but was back asleep almost at once. He didn't even budge when I slid my hand under the mattress, reassuring myself that Lisa's binder was still there.

The coffee was already gurgling and smelling fantastic when I emerged into the hallway and headed for the kitchen. "Thanks,

Dad," I said, giving him a kiss on the cheek.

"But of course," he said. "When do you think we can open this fridge?"

"Not yet," Mom said before I could answer. "Give it a chance to cool down first."

I shivered, rubbing my arms under the thick sweatshirt. "It can't have gotten very warm in there, if it's this cold out here. I should go start a fire."

"On it!" came Jen's cheerful voice from the living room.

I filled two mugs with coffee, added a generous portion of cream (yes, opening the fridge, probably endangering us all, so sue me) to each, and carried them down the hall. Jen was crouched in front of the fireplace, doing her magic.

"Where's your woodpile?" she asked, taking the mug I handed her with a look of undying gratitude. "Time to restock in here."

"On the back porch."

"No, I mean the real woodpile. That's only like three days' worth of firewood you've got back there."

"The real woodpile?" I echoed, stupidly.

Jen took a big swig of coffee and turned to give me a look. "Tell me you've got more wood than what's on your back porch, Cam."

"Um, I don't know?" I cast my mind over the Brixton estate, thinking about the various sheds and outbuildings and spaces I hadn't even really explored yet. "Maybe? We can just turn up the central heating, you know. I don't pay for it."

"Don't be silly." She added a final piece of kindling and began stacking firewood in a lattice pattern over it. "I don't know if you're aware, but periodically the power goes out here, some-times for many hours at a time."

"Ha ha," I said, sipping my coffee. Delicious.

"Besides, fire heat is soooo much better for you."

"In what way, exactly? And can't I just buy some more wood somewhere?" I didn't have a lot of spare cash, but how expensive could wood be? It literally grew on trees. And if there was one thing this island had, it was trees.

Jen rolled her eyes. "Good luck, this time of year. If you can find anything at all, you'll pay through the nose for it. And it won't be dry—might not even be seasoned."

"Hm." I watched as she finished laying the fire and lit a match to the bottom corner. The paper caught at once, the kindling fast behind it. It already felt warmer in the room, though I knew that was just the psychological effect of seeing the flames.

"Okay then." She sat back and admired her work a moment before joining me on the couch. "Good coffee."

"My dad made it."

"I am a man of many talents," Dad said, coming into the living room with a platter of toasted bagels. "Breakfast only one of them."

"One of the most important ones," I said, helping myself to a bagel heavily laden with cream cheese. "Should we let the camper boys know it's breakfast time?"

"Nah, let them sleep," Dad said. "There's plenty more where this came from."

"As well as about ten pounds of leftover turkey," Jen said.

I grimaced. "Turkey for breakfast? Ugh."

Mom came in then, with a cut-up bowl of fruit, and we once more turned our full attention to eating. After all, what was Thanksgiving weekend for?

❧

It was nearly eight o'clock before I heard the telltale sound of a sheriff SUV rolling down the driveway. I got up and checked out the window: just Kip, so far as I could tell.

"Well, show time, I guess," I said with a sigh. Sitting by Jen's crackling fire and enjoying a simple breakfast with her and my folks had been so pleasant. So…normal. I had the feeling that that was the last normal moment we were going to have for a while.

"Good morning, Ms. Tate," Kip said as I let him in.

I didn't even tease him about going all official on me, just offered him a cup of coffee.

"Thanks, that would be great. Black, please."

In the kitchen, I found that the four of us had already drained the first pot, so I ground the beans and started a second one. By the time I got back into the living room with his mug of black, Kip was pacing uncomfortably.

"Ah, thank you. Well, as I was just explaining to your folks here, we need to talk to each of you individually. Deputy Sherman is already over in the main house, getting set up."

"Deputy Sherman?" I hadn't met a Deputy Sherman. Come to think of it, I hadn't met a Deputy-Anyone-Other-Than-Kip. But of course Kip wouldn't be the only law enforcement in the county.

Jen smiled at Kip. "Ooh, an import all the way from Friday Harbor."

"Well." Kip looked even more uncomfortable; he drew himself taller, clutching his coffee mug. "There's a lot of you to question. Sheriff Fernandez wants this all done by the book."

"Who do you want to question first?" Jen asked. "And where do you want us?"

Kip shrugged. "Strictly speaking, we should have you all down to the station. But, well, that's got all kinds of logistical issues."

I nodded, thinking of the tiny station, and its even tinier interview room.

"So I'm going to have you all come over to the main house. We can use the Brixtons' breakfast room for our little chats, and I'll have the rest of you wait in the living room."

I tried to remember which one was the breakfast room. The house had so very many rooms…well, it had to be on the first floor. I hadn't spent much time on the first floor—or anywhere in the house, really. Caretaker though I was.

My parents started gathering their jackets for the oh-so-long walk to the house across the driveway. I put another log on the fire and lowered the flue a bit, so it would burn slower and hotter, then grabbed my own coat.

"Shouldn't there be more of you?" Kip asked, his voice dry. "Where's the rest of the gentlemen?"

"Oh, they're sleeping in the RV," I told him. "I can get them up."

"Thank you." Kip shepherded Jen and my parents over to the main house.

I knocked on the door of the Intruder. "Rise and shine, sleepy-heads!" I called. "Sheriffs are here."

The door opened and Kevin poked his head out. "We're up. Come on in, your brother's still getting dressed."

I climbed the metal steps into the absurd vehicle. A delicious aroma of coffee met me. "We have coffee in the house," I said, feeling a little defensive. I nodded at Colin, seated at the RV's kitchen table with a mug in front of him.

Kevin shrugged and smiled, his most adorable smile, just for my benefit, I knew it. I plunked down at the table across from Colin, who also gave me a smile. Not that I was comparing such things. Of course not.

"I had to try out my new Magnifetta," Kevin said, removing the carafe from a gigantic stainless-steel tank of a machine and pouring me a cup without asking. Adding just the right amount of cream without asking. I watched Colin notice this and not comment on it.

Smart man.

I considered not taking the coffee, out of principle, but it was coffee, which is a higher principle in and of itself. So.

"This is delicious," I had to admit, after taking a sip.

Kevin grinned. "I grabbed a bag of your local beans when I was in town. They're pretty good. The Magnifetta does a good job extracting all the flavor without crushing the delicate notes."

Over the rim of his own mug, I saw Colin's eyes dancing with merriment, but he remained silent. *Such* a smart man.

I nodded at him again, amusement in my own eyes I knew, and looked back at Kevin. Surely he knew we all found him ridiculous, with his excessive foodie-ism. And yet it didn't stop him. He loved cooking too much, and everything that went with it—for him, at least: finding just the right, weird, rare ingredients; hunting up the exact right recipes and methodologies for combining and preparing those ingredients; presenting them to an appreciative audience, even if that audience was often just himself. He wasn't a bad man. He just…needed to find someone to share this obsession with.

And that someone wasn't me.

Cliff emerged from somewhere in the back of the camper. "I smell coffee!" he said, cheerfully.

Kevin was already pouring him a cup, handing it to him black.

"We have to go to the main house to talk to the cops," I told my brother, "so drink up." I followed my own advice. Really, this coffee was head and shoulders above what Dad had brewed up in my little guesthouse.

There are some pieces of information we'd be better off without.

I sighed internally, mourning my last swallow of the delicious stuff as I handed the empty mug back to Kevin. "Thanks. So, we'd better get over there."

"We'll be right behind you," Cliff said, as Colin got up to accompany me.

"Interesting ex-boyfriend you got there," Colin said, as soon as we were alone on the driveway. I arched an eyebrow at him, but he laughed before I could say anything. "And yes, I know I have an interesting ex as well. Guess we're even."

I laughed as well. "Even. Yes."

And then we were at the front door of the Brixtons' house. Right where I'd been just a few short hours ago, talking and drinking with JoJo in the middle of the night, before my trip to the boat to retrieve Lisa's binder. Suddenly I felt very, very tired all over again, even with my successful mission. Was this ever going to be all solved and settled?

Colin brushed a gentle hand against the small of my back. It could almost have been accidental; I felt it there and then gone, quick as a moment. Much more lingering was the feeling of friendship and peace it gave me. And maybe a little something warmer, but I couldn't think about that right now.

"Good, come on in," Kip said, opening the door at my knock. "Find a seat in here; we'll call you when it's your turn."

Colin and I joined the others in the large sitting room—front parlor—ballroom—whatever. It looked like a Pacific Northwest version of an Agatha Christie movie, with the crazy jumbled assortment of folks on all this fine furniture. Mom and Dad sat together on an elegant loveseat; Clary and Maxine had taken a matching one across from them, sitting demonstrably close to one another. JoJo slouched in an overstuffed brocade chair, sipping his own cup of undoubtedly inferior-to-Kevin's coffee. Diana and Emmett Brixton sat at either end of a long sofa under the front window, far enough apart that another person or two could sit comfortably between them.

I led Colin to a pair of smaller brocade chairs close to the unlit fireplace. There was still room for seven or eight more people in here, if Kip wanted to round up more suspects. Okay, five or six—Kevin and Cliff came in and took a different pair of brocade chairs, in a darker, but of course coordinating, color.

As soon as they'd sat down, Lisa Cannon walked into the room from the hallway; a young woman in a sheriff's uniform was just behind her, as if escorting her. Lisa gave me a cordial nod without really seeming to single me out, and turned to look at the deputy. "Is that all?"

"Please take a seat, Ms. Cannon; we may need to ask another question or two," the woman said.

"Of course," Lisa murmured, and sat on the sofa between the Brixtons, continuing to not really meet my eye. I was dying to talk to her—alone, of course—to let her know what had happened last night, that I'd found the binder, that it was safe in my house…well, it would just have to wait.

Kip and the new deputy—she must be Sherman—consulted briefly before Kip turned to the room at large and said, "Ms. Liu, would you come with us?"

Maxine drew herself slowly up from the loveseat. Clary patted her arm as she got to her feet and whispered something I couldn't hear. Maxine nodded, frowning, and followed the deputies out.

We all sat silently for a minute or two, unsure of the protocol. I could see Diana Brixton looking more uncomfortable than most of the rest of us; did she feel like she ought to offer us all coffee, or breakfast, or something? Were we really all supposed to sit here in this one room? I guessed so.

Lisa, clearly picking up on Diana's unease, turned and began engaging her in conversation. From what I could hear, it seemed to be just pleasant chitchat about nothing, though I did notice a brittleness to her tone, her smile.

Well, she must be at least as exhausted and unsettled as I was. And curious about what I'd found last night. Anyway, who knew how her questioning had gone?

Even so, her words to Diana broke the ice. My parents began murmuring to each other as Cliff said something to Kevin. I turned to Colin. "Not exactly how I'd imagined spending today."

He smiled. "Not much ever does go as expected, does it?"

After about fifteen minutes, Deputy Sherman led Maxine back into the room. She practically fled back to the loveseat and curled up in Clary's arms. I glanced over at Diana Brixton, who was very carefully not watching her daughter with her lover.

"Clarice Brixton, please," said Deputy Sherman.

Clary gave Maxine one last squeeze before getting up and following the deputy out of the room.

I glanced around, taking a quick count. At this rate, we'd be here all morning, at least.

My mom was clearly making the same calculation. "I hope we don't miss that twelve twenty-five ferry," she said.

"You will," came Kip's voice from the doorway, "I'm sorry. We're going to need everyone to stay on. This is just preliminary questioning we're doing now."

We all turned and gaped at him. "What...why?" I blurted out. "Wasn't that woman's death an accident?"

He took a few steps into the room, shaking his head gently. He looked sad, and stressed, and something else I couldn't quite figure out. "I don't recall telling you anything of the sort, Ms. Tate."

I glanced over at Maxine, but she was avoiding looking at anyone.

"I...just thought I heard that?" I said to Kip, uncertain. "That she slipped and hit her head and fell into the water?"

"We do not have a cause of death at this time," Kip said, to me and to the room at large. "We've been asked to keep all witnesses and potential witnesses here for further questioning."

"But—how long is this going to be?" my brother asked, looking suddenly worried. "I've got to get to SeaTac tonight; my flight to Bangkok leaves first thing tomorrow morning."

"Asked by who?" Jen added.

Kip looked even more unhappy as he answered Cliff, ignoring Jen's question. "That is all I can tell you at this time. If I were you, I'd see about getting that flight shifted."

"Well, this is madness!" Diana Brixton protested. "We had planned to leave the island today as well; I've got a brunch in Bellevue tomorrow."

"I'm sorry, Mrs. Brixton. I'm doing all I can." With that, he left the room, heading back down the hall to where Deputy Sherman had taken Clary.

We all looked around at each other, stunned and unhappy. From between the Brixtons, Lisa Cannon gave me a small encouraging smile. I tried to send her a telepathic message, but of course I didn't possess *that* useful superpower. "At least we all have plenty to eat, hmm?" she said, brightly. "Houses full of Thanksgiving leftovers."

Diana looked at her as though she'd lost her mind, then just shook her head and stared out the window.

Time passed. JoJo was called next, and then Jen. When she came back and Colin was called, I asked her, "So, how did it go?"

She shrugged. "Nothing unusual, really. They just asked me to tell them everything that happened, from when we all first went down there to light the bonfire. They made me tell it all two or three times, and Sherman jotted everything down in her little notebook."

"Usually Kip does that," I said.

Jen smiled. "He outranks her; she has to do the note-taking for now, till the department hires someone newer, at least."

"What do they think happened?"

Maxine put in, "I told you what I heard. I think now they're just trying to be sure they've covered their asses in case any high-er-ups come in and question everything. You know how it is when too many people start dying."

"How it is? Like, here? Or on TV?"

"On TV. No one ever dies here."

It was nearly noon before I was called back—the second to last person. For some reason, I was very nervous. But I wasn't even a witness, much less a participant. What did I have to worry about?

It was the waiting, I told myself. And this unknown Deputy Sherman, all the way from Friday Harbor, two islands away.

Kip ushered me into the bright, cozy breakfast room—bigger than my entire kitchen, but it did fit the house—and had me take a seat at the small table. "Coffee?" He indicated an indus-trial-style carafe and a stack of paper cups on the sideboard, next to Diana Brixton's elegant silver tea service, polished to a high sheen. The effect was as if a mongrel mutt had wandered into a posh dog show and squatted on stage.

"No, thanks, I've already had several cups." Probably I wouldn't be able to drink regular coffee again, after Kevin's amazing Magnetotron-stuff, or whatever it was. I certainly wouldn't be able to stomach cop coffee, I knew that.

"All right, then, let's get started." Kip sat opposite me; Deputy Sherman was at the far end of the table, turning her notebook over to a fresh page. I took a moment to study her as Kip set up his little tape recorder. She was very young—though she probably wasn't quite as young as she looked, because if I didn't know better, I'd say she was seventeen, and cops aren't seventeen. Short dark hair, professionally cut and gleamingly clean. I felt a tiny pang of envy; not everyone could pull off an Audrey Hepburn pixie, and as a hairdresser I was painfully aware of that fact. But she was pretty enough, in a quiet way, that it worked. Dark eyes, small nose, and a trim figure; her uniform fit her just right, without being ostentatious.

"So," Kip began. "Starting with the decision to go light a bonfire on the beach yesterday afternoon, tell us what happened."

It went just as Jen had said. I walked them through the whole thing, such as it was. Kip stopped me a few times for clarification, even though he'd actually been there the whole time. We slowed down a bit when I went over how Jen, Colin and I had gone down to inspect the body, but even there, I hadn't much to add. I gave as good a description as I could—same as I'd given Kip before—of seeing the woman prowling around on the boat. "The woman on the beach could be the same person, but I can't be a hundred percent sure," I concluded. "I never saw her all that clearly when she was alive."

"And it was dark," Kip allowed. "So what happened next?"

I took them through to the end of the day pretty quickly, there really being nothing else noteworthy to tell. "And then I went to bed, kind of early," I told them. "I was exhausted, and done being social."

"You are somewhat of an introvert," Kip said, kindly. Deputy Sherman glanced up at him for a moment before returning her attention to her notebook.

"Yeah. This whole weekend…I mean, even without the deaths…it's been a bit out of my comfort zone." I smiled at them both.

Kip had leaned forward to turn off his tape recorder but then paused and looked up at me. "So you went to bed, a bit early. Did you sleep through the night, or did anything else happen?"

My heart pounded, my arms tingled, I was going to vanish, oh crap! This had totally blindsided me. What did he know?! How did he know it? Had somebody seen me? "Um, yeah—I mean, mostly. I…um, found my cat in the middle of the night. I mean, he found me; he came back and meowed outside the window and I got up and let him in. You know he was missing all day. I'd been worried, but he's fine." Now I was babbling, and I knew my face was turning red. I rubbed my arms, trying to keep the feeling in them, trying to stay visible. "But other than that, no."

Kip watched me closely. Deputy Sherman scribbled notes.

"You didn't see anything when you got up in the night?" Kip asked, at last. "Other than your cat, I mean?"

Oh crap, I suddenly realized. Had JoJo told them I'd come over for a flashlight? Why was I lying, even? No crime in borrowing a flashlight. *Crap!* Too late now. "No. Nothing. I mean, the cat, but, yeah. Nothing else." *Shut up, Cam, stop talking.*

"Which door did you let him in by?"

"What?"

"The front door or the back door. You said you heard him outside your bedroom window, correct?"

"Yeah."

"Your bedroom, if I am correct in my assumption, is just about at the middle of your residence. Did you go to the front door or the back door to let the cat in?"

My mind raced. The back door looked down to the beach; the

front door looked to the driveway and the main house. "Um, the front door. I went to the front door."

Deputy Sherman's hand moved across the page of her notebook. Kip nodded. "Ms. Jennifer Darling was sleeping in your living room, on the couch, is that correct?"

"Yes—but, she didn't wake up, I don't think. I heard her snoring. I tried to be quiet, I don't think she heard me."

"Of course." He watched me a moment longer, his eyes revealing nothing. "All right, Ms. Tate, that will be all for now. Thank you."

And just like that, I was released from my questioning. I walked back to the Brixtons' living room on shaky legs, taking my seat again by Jen. She reached over and squeezed my hand briefly.

Cliff got called after me; he was the last person. The cops kept him even less time than they'd kept the others.

"All right, that's all for now," Kip announced to the room when he escorted my brother back. "You don't have to stay right here, but I'd appreciate it if no one left the island until I give you the say-so. And please stay in cell phone range, wherever you go." He was using pretty words like "please" and "appreciate", but his tone made it clear that compliance was not voluntary.

I wanted to point out that cell phones barely worked even here on the Brixton estate, but I didn't want to sound snotty, so I just nodded.

"I'll be in town, and you have my number," Lisa said to Kip at once, rising gracefully to her feet. She was out the door before I could even catch her eye once more. I really, really needed to talk to her...when were all these *people* going to be allowed to leave?

I stifled my frustration. "Well, I'll just be back home," I told Kip. "With anyone who wants to hang out there with me."

"It's not like we have much choice," my mom pointed out. Their ferry must be pulling out right now, without them on it. I hoped they could get reservations for later, or tomorrow—assuming Kip would ever let us all go. The later it got on this holiday weekend, the harder it would be to get on any ferry. At least my parents were retired. If Cliff missed his flight, he was really going to be up a creek.

I led a little procession back around to my guesthouse: my parents and brother, Jen, Colin, Kevin. "Is anyone hungry?" Kevin asked. "I could make up some…"

I didn't even stick around to see what amazing thing he was going to create now. "I'm going to look for some more firewood," I told the others, and walked straight through my house to the back door, and out again.

For a few minutes, I just walked aimlessly around in the little woods behind the house, breathing and decompressing and waiting for my skin to stop itching. Not because of chameleoning this time; just the general discomfort of being around too many people, for too long. How had I lived in Seattle for so many years? Had I truly adapted to quiet island life this fast? God, I didn't think I could ever ride a bus or walk on a crowded sidewalk again.

At this rate, I was going to be a wild-haired old hermit before I turned thirty.

After a few minutes, I'd relaxed enough to actually do what I'd said I'd come out here for. There was a small shed, or maybe lean-to, not far behind my guesthouse. It didn't even have a real door, just an opening. Inside were large empty terra cotta pots, a few half-emptied bags of soil and mulch, and some gardening tools—a rusty rake, a short-handled shovel, things like that. I thought I'd noticed a stack of firewood in here earlier, but upon closer inspection, it was just a pile of old lumber. Like if a deck had been torn down and replaced. We could still burn this, though, right? Had it been treated with weird chemicals or anything? I'd have to ask Jen, or Colin.

I looked out behind the shed, but no firewood here either. What about the larger outbuilding by the main house?

But I didn't want to go poking through there, with the Brixtons home. Any firewood there would be for the use of the main house. But I'd check it out, after they were gone, whenever that would be.

The guesthouse didn't have a garage, but it did have a sort of overhang on the roadward side, hemmed in by trees and not very inviting. I checked under there; nothing.

Stymied, but ready to face human beings again, I walked back to the house.

And that's when I noticed the latest gift.

Three big ziplock bags leaned against the side of the back porch. Had I missed them on my way out? Or…had they been put there while I was out here?

Impossible—I'd have seen anyone walking around back here.

Maybe when I was around the side of the house? But I'd only been there ten or fifteen seconds, tops.

My hands, my entire arms trembled as I bent down to look at the bags. They were labeled, quite unnecessarily, in the precise but shaky handwriting of an older person: WHITE TURKEY MEAT, DARK TURKEY MEAT, HOMEMADE CRANBERRY SAUCE. The sauce was a bright jumble of red and orange; the meat was neatly sliced.

Who the devil leaves anonymous Thanksgiving leftovers for someone??!

"Meow," said James, appearing from somewhere and sniffing interestedly at the bag of dark meat.

"No way, dude," I told him, picking up the bags. "A zucchini is one thing; I'm not eating meat and sauce that came out of some psycho's kitchen, and neither are you." I'd throw them away in the house, sealing up the trash can tightly. "Come on, I'll give you some cat food." And probably some of *our* leftover turkey, the poor kitty. Maybe if I gave him more treats, he'd stop wandering off and scaring me half to death all the time.

I took a final deep breath before pushing open the back door. James scrambled between my feet and darted into the kitchen, where Kevin was apparently putting the finishing touches on some open-faced sandwiches before popping them into the oven. "What's that?" he asked, nodding at the bags. "I could—"

"Nope and nope," I said, heading straight for the trash. "You may be a food genius but even you cannot redeem culinary assault."

"I...what?"

"Long story," I muttered. "But we're not eating this."

"All right." I could just feel him dying to ask more, but being careful, oh so careful around me. Sigh. I left him to his foodie tasks and went to the front room, hoping to pull Jen aside so I could tell her the latest; I did *not* want to involve everyone else in this nonsense.

"How did your firewood search go?" she asked.

I told her about the lumber. "But I'm no expert," I said. "I'll want you to look at it."

"You're probably right, we wouldn't want to burn that. Let's go check it out now," she said, getting the point immediately.

Once outside, I led her to the shed while I told her about the latest "gift". "Ugh, that's disturbing," she said.

"Yeah. What the heck is going on?"

"I want to see that handwriting," she said. "This is the first time there's any kind of note, right?"

"I threw the bags away."

"Well, pull them out of the trash. Cam! This is a clue, come on."

I sighed. "What, Kip's got a database of local wackadoodles' handwriting samples and he's going to put everything else aside to identify this culprit for me? Hey, maybe the Friday Harbor cops want to chime in on it. Inter-island food-gifting incident!"

"You can't pretend you think this isn't all related somehow. Trespassing, prowling, stalking—dead bodies all over the place— honey, this isn't normal."

"You're telling me."

"So..."

I sighed. "Okay, we'll dig out the bags and tell Kip about it. But not right now!" I hastened to add. "I can't do all this while my family's here. They're already worried enough about me."

She stood at the shed doorway, giving me a hard look. "Cam, *I'm* worried about you. Let me say it again: this is not normal. Not normal for Orcas Island—not normal for anywhere. You could be in danger. You've been in danger. Somebody's focused on you in a weird, weird way."

Well, when she put it that way... "I'll see if I can talk to Kip without anyone hovering over me when I do it."

"Of course you can." She rolled her eyes. "What did we just spend all morning doing? Talking to Kip not in front of other people."

"All right, all right."

"Good." She turned and glanced into the shed. "You're right, don't burn that indoors. We should have taken it down to the beach for the bonfire last night."

"Okay, thanks." We headed back to the house. "So where *do* I get more firewood now?"

"I don't know, hon. Let me ask around. Most folks stock up in the summer or early fall. If anyone's still got wood for sale, you'll pay a premium, for sure."

I wondered if Diana Brixton would cover the costs...nah, probably not. I looked around us, at the dense forest. "Maybe someone could cut down a tree or two here?"

Jen snorted. "You're kidding, right? Are you that much of a city girl?"

"What?" I asked, a little stung.

"Even if you could find someone to do that right now, that would be no good for you. Wood has to season—to dry out. It needs a year or more after being cut down. Ever try to light a fire with wet wood?"

"Oh." Now that she mentioned it, I did seem to remember something about "green" wood. Maybe from a story I'd read.

"Yes, I am a city girl," I told her. "Be gentle. This is all new to me."

She smiled as we reached the back door. "Sorry. You just seem like you belong here; I forget you haven't always been here."

All my earlier pique vanished in an instant. "Thanks." I pulled her into a quick hug, surprising her, but she returned it with equal warmth.

"So let's see those bags," she said, releasing me.

In the kitchen, Kevin's sandwiches were in the oven, releasing a powerfully fantastic aroma. Fortunately, Kevin himself had vacated the premises, leaving us a clear shot at the trashcan, unobserved. I pushed aside James's empty food bowl and opened the cabinet under the sink.

"Here you go." I handed Jen the bag of white meat and the cranberry sauce, then dug around for the dark meat. It had slipped to the bottom of the bag, and was covered with something slimy and awful. "Yech."

"Hmm." She ignored my distress, focusing on the handwriting. "Old person."

"Yeah, I can see that."

"It looks more feminine than masculine, but I can't really be sure." She frowned at the bags. "All older people were taught cursive like that, so it could be an old dude."

Ephraim Snooks had been an old dude. But he was dead, the day before Thanksgiving. Before making any leftovers.

Jen went on, her eyes vacant as her mind traveled. "Then again, that doesn't really narrow anything down. Nine-tenths of this island is old folks. So the question remains: who? And why?"

"Yes," I agreed. "The question remains."

We stared at each other for a minute. "Well," she said at last, "let's get these bags to Kip. Do you want to call him, or shall I?"

"Should we dump the food out first, clean the bags?" I could just see myself hauling nasty leftovers to town...

"Don't!" she cried. "What if it's poison? He'll need to test that—it's more evidence!"

"Is everything all right in there?" Mom's voice wafted down the hall.

"We're fine!" I squealed, giving Jen a panicked look. "Just… working on my play!"

Jen stifled a giggle, shaking her head. "Good save."

"Thanks." I glanced again at the awful bags on the counter. "I guess we could put them in a grocery bag or something."

"Right." She rummaged around under the sink, found one, and began loading them up. "You should call Kip. You're the one who found them."

"Okay." I patted my pockets. "I must have left my phone in my room. Be right back."

James was again snoozing in my unmade bed. "Eat and sleep, is that all you know how to do?" I asked my silly cat. He opened one eye, gave me a look that said *You wanna make something of it?*, then closed it again. "You're lucky I don't make the bed over you, cat," I said.

My phone was on my nightstand, just where I'd left it. I picked it up and was about to leave when I realized I was alone. Perfect chance to call Lisa.

I slid my hand under the mattress, to reassure myself that her binder was still there…and my fingers found nothing.

My heart pounded, my skin flared and tingled. I reached in further, thrusting my hand higher, then lower—and there it was. Down closer to my feet than I'd remembered. "Oh jeez," I whispered, sinking to the floor in desperate relief.

James snorted with indignation and hopped to the floor beside me, his slumber so rudely disturbed by my fussing with the bed.

"Sorry, dude," I said to him, rumpling his ears as I tried to catch my breath and slow my terrified heartbeat. "I know you were guarding it, you little watch cat. You wouldn't let anything happen here."

I wished I could truly believe that.

CHAPTER 12

Finally fully composed, I sat back on the bed and punched in Lisa's number, but it rang and rang and eventually went to voice mail. "Hey Lisa," I said, "I've got some info on that project we were talking about the other day. Let me know when you have a few minutes and I'll run over and update you. Thanks!" I hung up, clutching my phone. I hoped that wasn't too casual, that she'd know this was important.

Of course she'd know. She must be dying to get this binder back.

I put my fingers under the mattress again. Yep, still there.

Now I punched in Kip's number, getting his voice mail as well. "Hey Kip," I said after the beep. "There's been a new development. I mean, not a big one; no need to rush over here or anything. Just another little weird thing that you should know about. Call me when you get a chance."

Jeez, where was everybody? Well, they'd call me back.

What if Lisa called when I wasn't alone? I'd just have to deal with it. I was tempted to call again right now, but I didn't want to be a pest.

I wished I could tell Jen about the binder.

Wait. Was this just my instinctive, knee-jerk reaction? *Could* I tell Jen?

I had spent my whole life hiding from the scary things. Quite literally. And as I'd been learning so painfully recently, this was not working. My big insight, just last week, had been about the need for connection. Friends. Allies.

I needed an ally—in life in general, and with this situation in particular. A person I could really trust, who would believe me, would believe *in* me. Someone to whom I could reveal my supernatural disability—because without them knowing that, I would always be covering something up. I had thought that person might be Kevin…but that had been a horrible mistake. Sure, he was being all friendly and sweet and apologetic now, but that was clearly because he had decided my confession had been, I don't know, a moment of temporary insanity on my part? And because he wanted something? How else to explain why he wanted to get back together, while making no mention of the details of that horrible evening when it all fell apart between us?

There was my brother Cliff, of course, who I trusted completely, even though we'd never really talked about this directly. He'd grown up with me; he'd seen more than anyone else. It would be a small leap to tell him about it in plain words, to have this overt between us. But though he loved me, he lived on the other side of the world. He could not be here for me. And I didn't see myself running away to Thailand. I'd already run away far enough.

No, I was determined to not leave Orcas, at least not until I'd uncovered the truth about whatever nest of snakes had made itself at home here. And I couldn't do that alone. What it all boiled down to was that it was time to reveal myself to someone on the island, someone who cared about this place as much as I had come to. Someone who could handle the truth about Cam Tate, human chameleon.

Much as I liked and admired her, I knew that that person could not be Lisa. Yes, we were building a relationship of closeness and trust, but things were still too imbalanced. Though I was doing her a huge favor right now, I was nowhere near the point of being able to reveal such weirdness and vulnerability to her. My growing friendship with her depended on her seeing me becoming stronger and more capable—not on me being a freaky weirdo who would never fit in anywhere.

So it all came back to Jen. Warm, open, accepting Jen.

I should walk back into that kitchen and tell her everything...

Except I couldn't, I realized with a sinking heart. Not now, not yet. This binder, and everything it represented, was Lisa Cannon's business, not mine, and she had sworn me to secrecy. I couldn't tell Jen about it, or about my sneaking aboard Snooks's boat or anything. Not without breaking Lisa's trust. At the very least, I had to talk to Lisa first.

"Come on, call me back," I whispered to Lisa. James rubbed against my ankles and then jumped up on the bed. I scritched his ears absently.

My phone sat silent in my hands.

Jen was waiting for me in the kitchen.

Why did I always have to be so alone in everything? A house full of people, and here I was hiding in my bedroom.

Well. I couldn't hide all day. "Okay, kitty, time to go," I said to James, who had somehow insinuated himself into my lap and was three-quarters of the way to falling asleep once more. Acting nothing like a cat who had been locked under the floorboards of a boat and left to die. Ah, the resilience of youth. Squaring my shoulders, I got up and tucked my phone in my pocket, set the cat down, and opened my bedroom door.

Jen was right there. "Well?" she asked.

"Cripes," I said. "Were you waiting here in the hall for me or what?"

She laughed. "I just came to check on you, and you walked out. So? Did you get hold of Kip?"

"Left a message," I said.

"Huh," she said. "All right. I guess he is busy."

"He'll call back," I assured her. "I told him there was a new development. That's cop-nip if ever there was."

She snorted with laughter.

"Sandwiches are ready!" Kevin called, from the kitchen.

Okay, I totally did not want to get back together with him, but in that moment, I was super grateful he was here.

☙

Of course the sandwiches were freaking delicious. We all ate them in my tiny living room, by the roaring fire, because sometime between when Jen and I had come in from "looking at the firewood" and now, it had started to pour outside. "Welcome to the San Juans," I muttered around a mouthful. "If you don't like the weather, wait five minutes."

"Really oughta go check on my boat after lunch," Colin said. "Hadn't intended to leave her overnight like that." He stood by my front door, staring out at the rain.

"Kip said we could go any time, as long as we stayed in cell range," I pointed out. So where *was* Lisa? Not in cell range to me, anyway. I tried not to let my inner turmoil show on my face.

Colin turned and gave me his adorable grin as he held up his own half-eaten sandwich. "Wasn't going to leave before this," he said. "Kev's been talking about them all morning."

"Ah." I smiled back at him, and then at Kevin, who beamed back.

"See? I'm good for something," Kevin said.

Jen raised her eyebrows but said nothing.

"Home run every time," my dad murmured appreciatively over his own sandwich. He looked up at me. I could almost feel him wanting to poke at me, about why I wasn't still dating this marvelous man, why I wasn't willing to give him another chance; but to his credit, he held back. And so did everyone else.

But I know they were all thinking it.

"You cooked, I'll clean up," I said to Kevin, gathering up everyone's empty plates. Old habits die hard; but also, it was really only fair.

Jen followed me into the kitchen. "Nothing from Kip yet?"

I pulled out my phone, casually shielding the screen from her as I glanced at it in case I'd somehow missed a call from Lisa. But no. Nothing. "Nope."

She sighed. "Try him again."

I shook my head, stuffing my phone back in my pocket and starting to rinse the dishes. The baking sheet Kevin had toasted the sandwiches on was a total greasy mess. No wonder they had been so delicious; there must be a quart of olive oil on here. "I don't want to pester him. Come on, Jen, you know he'll call when he can."

She gave a second, more dramatic sigh. "And it has to be *raining*, on top of everything else! We're just locked up here all day and can't do *anything!*"

I couldn't help myself, I giggled at her. "Does someone need something to do, maybe?"

"We've *got* something to do! We've got mysterious deaths to investigate!"

"I thought that's what the cops were for," said Colin, poking his head through the kitchen doorway. "Give it a rest, Darling." He looked at me. "Gonna head off to the marina, check on things. I can come back whenever I'm needed."

"Sure thing."

He nodded, buttoning up his jacket. "Cell service is usually pretty good there."

"Oh god, let me come with you," Jen said to him. "I have to get out of here, I'm going completely stir-crazy."

I wanted to protest, but actually, it was probably for the best if she cleared out for a little while. Especially if Lisa ever got back to me.

I did so look forward to being able to stop hiding things from Jen.

"Have fun, you two," I said, continuing to load plates in the dishwasher.

"I'll call you in an hour or so," Jen said to me. "But call me *at once* if you hear anything."

"Will do." She followed Colin back down the hallway, and I felt one little piece of the tension in my chest release a little.

That is, until I cleared enough of the dishes off the counter to see a grocery bag next to the fridge. I peered inside, only to find the ziplock bags of food, neatly labeled with the mystery-old-person handwriting.

Who was *stalking* me like this?

I wanted so badly to dump the food out, but Jen was right; the authorities had to at least be given the opportunity to look at it before we trashed it. Kip had better call back soon. These weren't getting any fresher.

At least I could put them in the fridge.

Or...I could have if the fridge weren't so completely stuffed with leftovers, and food we hadn't even gotten around to opening, and beer, and cider, and and and...

With a sigh, I tucked the grocery bag back out on the back porch, behind a flowerpot. It was still cold enough out there. And what, I was worried about the creepy un-asked-for probably-poisonous food spoiling?

I started the dishwasher and looked around the kitchen to see if there was more cleanup I ought to be doing, before finally admitting to myself that I was still avoiding people. People who had come all this way to see me. And most of whom I had actually invited, or—in the case of my brother—would have invited if I'd had any clue that he might come all the way across the world.

So I checked my phone one last time (no call from Lisa, no calls from anyone), and headed out to the living room.

Where I found my parents, brother, and Kevin gathered around a Scrabble board. And drinking spiced cider.

It was so much like my thwarted vision that I didn't know whether to laugh or cry. All they needed were hand-knit sweaters.

"Hey, there you are," Dad said. "Come team up with me, I need a pinch-hitter. They're killing me here."

"No fair!" cried my brother. "She's a writer now, she has *all* the words."

I squeezed next to my dad, sharing his chair; he shifted aside for me. "Hmm…you could make…" And I leaned in and whispered in his ear.

"Oooh yes," he said, laying the tiles out and scoring us a neat thirty-two points.

"Are we going to allow this?" Cliff appealed to our mom.

"I don't see why not," she said, giving me a warm glance. "It's not like we can add her as a separate player this late in the game."

"It's okay with me," Kevin said, still trying to ingratiate himself, I'm sure.

Whatever. I'd take it. "Great. So, let's see what else we get here," I said, reaching into the draw pile for new tiles.

ॐ

It was a super fun game. So much fun that we played another. Dad and I won both times. Then Kevin made us all a little snack, and some more spiced cider.

I was heading back to the kitchen with yet another pile of dirty dishes when I felt my phone buzz in my pocket. *Yes!* I thought, rushing to set down the dishes.

"Lisa," I breathed into the phone, once I'd dug it out. "Thank goodness. I've got the—"

"Cam, darling, hello!" she sang out, her voice false and brittle, an imitation of delight. She almost sounded like Diana Brixton. I could hear voices in the background—ah, so she wasn't alone, she was trying to be subtle. "So sorry to leave you hanging all day."

"That's okay!" I rushed to reassure her. "I just wanted to let you know I, um, got the thing and everything's fine." I could be subtle too. Yep, just like in the movies.

"That's great! I'm so happy to hear that." Now there was at least a little of her genuine warmth, amid the fake sparkle in her tone.

I walked over to the window, where the signal was better.

"What do you want me to do with it?"

"Please hang onto it for now. I'll be in touch next week and we can go from there."

"Next week?" I gaped at the phone. "But—"

"Nothing to worry about!" She practically shouted the words, though I could tell she was still trying to sound casual, cheerful. "I've got a bit much on my plate right now. *You know.* Thanks again!"

And then she hung up on me.

"Okay, that was *too weird*," I whispered, staring out the window as if I could see her house through the Brixtons' main house, and the trees, and the distance.

Was she okay? She sure sounded like she was trying to make me *think* she was okay.

Well, she had to be super relieved, at least. But clearly she was somewhere where she couldn't talk about it openly. I would just do as she asked: hang onto the binder and wait to hear more.

I stifled the urge to go put my hands under the mattress again. I knew it was still there; at least someone had been in the house all day, usually lots of us.

But I had so many questions. Was she ever going to answer them?

Wasn't she eager to get the binder back? Didn't she need it to manage her secret finances or something?

With a sigh, I shoved my phone back in my pocket and went back to cleanup.

☙

The afternoon wore on. Mom took a nap. I lazed around on my bed, trying to read, not really getting anywhere. Lisa didn't call again.

Then Colin called, wondering if we'd heard anything about whether we'd be questioned again soon, or really anything at all. I said no, we hadn't.

Then Jen called, wondering all the same things Colin had wondered. "Kip never called you back at all?" she asked, incredulous.

"No," I said. "That is strange. I'll try him again."

I got immediate voice mail for him this time. I left a casual, chirpy message, and immediately second-guessed myself as soon as I hung up, so I called again and left a more serious one, though trying not to sound too dire or anything, because it wasn't any kind of an emergency, of course, even though I'd now called three times about the same thing.

But why hadn't he called me back? That was very unlike him.

I wondered if I should check over at the main house, to see if any news had arrived there. But it was cold outside, and it just seemed *so far*. Anyway, someone would tell us if there was something we needed to know, right? JoJo, at the very least, would seize any excuse to get out of the house.

I wished I could nap, like Mom.

It got dark. Kevin made us all some dinner.

Nobody called, or left more leftovers, or anything.

"Well," said my dad, as we sat around in the living room. I was full again, antsy and bored and uneasy.

We all were.

"More Scrabble?" I asked.

Everyone shrugged noncommittally. Even Kevin looked dispirited. Nobody moved to set up the board.

"I wonder if we will be allowed to leave tomorrow," Mom said. I could see she was trying not to sound grumpy. She mostly succeeded.

I wanted to apologize—to her, to everyone—but what had *I* done? Just…invited them here. I didn't know there would be so much intrigue. And then so much nothing.

"Well, I might hit the hay," Kevin said at last, getting up and stretching.

My dad yawned. "Yeah. That's probably the best way to get things rolling again—get all cozy in bed."

So that's what we did. We all went to bed.

When it was midnight and I hadn't fallen asleep yet, I got up, switched on my light, and checked my phone again. Was it malfunctioning? No, it still looked like it worked, and had its stupid little one bar of service.

I switched off the phone's screen and lay there, worrying. Running the phone call with Lisa over in my mind. She'd sounded so very strange. Panicked? No, I'd seen her panicked; this was something else.

She was clearly stressed, though.

And then there was that *you know*. When she'd said she had a lot on her plate right now. There was a weird emphasis there... was she trying to tell me something?

Oh, my god. *Was* she?

What did I "know"? Or more to the point, what did I know, that Lisa knew I knew?

I knew her house had been broken into. But everyone knew that.

I knew something very important, that her crazy ex-husband would desperately want, had been stolen. And, so far as I was aware, only I knew that.

There'd been voices in the background when she called me. I'd assumed it was her usual troupe of actors. But what if it wasn't? What if she was in some kind of trouble?

I wished I'd paid more attention to those voices. They'd been animated; had they been angry, or having fun, or what?

Should I walk over to her house and see if she was all right? She had never hung up on me before. The whole short conversation had been too peculiar, from start to finish.

But if she wasn't all right...what could I do about it? Wouldn't I be putting myself in danger too? I'd spent twenty years avoiding that any way I could. Staying safe was all I cared about. *At some point that stopped mattering to you, Cam. What's going on with you?* I asked myself, and sighed heavily, because I was already getting dressed and grabbing JoJo's flashlight.

This island will be the death of me, I thought. *But I care too much about the people here to curl up in a ball and disappear.*

It was just freezing outside. I shivered, pulling my coat tighter around me and telling myself I needed to buy a thicker one, then paused on the back porch.

Something was different.

I looked at the nearly depleted pile of firewood, the groceries we'd stashed out here and hadn't used yet, an unopened case of beer...

The bag with the leftovers was missing.

Had my mysterious stalker-benefactor come by, seen them here, been offended, and taken them back?

Good riddance, I thought, but could not shake the unease I felt. I did *not* like someone prowling around here night and day. I had to get to the bottom of this.

I shook my head, and started out again, across the backyard, around the guesthouse, past the dark, silent Intruder. The main house was dark and quiet as well.

The path between the two estates was the darkest and quietest yet.

I emerged into the tiny clearing leading to Lisa's front door and paused, shining my flashlight up to her steps and porch. Something...right about eye level...reflected back at me; I moved the beam of the light back to where I'd seen it, but couldn't find anything.

I took a hesitant step forward, aiming the beam again. Nothing. My skin tingled. I tried to clear my throat, very softly; no sound emerged.

Just turn around and go home and call the cops if you're worried about her, I told myself, but now I couldn't move. Because there was someone lurking in the pitch dark on Lisa Cannon's porch. Even as I was admitting that fact to myself, a light flared up, blinding me: a giant flashlight, far more powerful than my own.

Like, as powerful as a police flashlight.

"Well, Cam," came Kip's mellifluous voice, pitched low and soft in the velvety night. "What an interesting development."

Kip. He was as safe as it got. Relieved that I wasn't going to chameleon, I drew in a big breath and walked the last few steps toward her porch. "Oh Kip," I said. "I've been trying to get a hold of you." He met me at the bottom of the steps, aiming his flashlight to the ground and then switching it off.

I struggled to see his face, keeping my flashlight low so as not to blind him, even though my own eyes were still adjusting to the after effects of that blinding glare.

"Let's go for a little walk," he said, still almost sotto voce. Before I could agree, he took my not-wounded arm and guided me further down onto the lawn. Toward Lisa's stairway-path to the beach. "Away from the house," he said. "Where we can talk."

This was weird. "Is everything all right?" I whispered. My heart rate skipped upward, and my skin tingled on my chest and belly. "What's going on? Where's Lisa?"

His hand tightened on my upper arm, almost painfully. "She's fine. Just walk."

I bit my lip, concentrating on not stumbling down the stairs. And on staying present. *This is Kip,* I told myself. *You trust him. He's safe.*

We emerged onto Lisa's beach. It was a tiny bit less dark down there, with the big expanse of water in front of us. There was still no moon, but the stars gave some light, where they weren't blocked by clouds. I could barely see Snooks's boat, bumping gently against the dock. Even the bright yellow police line tape was almost invisible.

But I could tell that Kip was trying to take me there.

I stopped in my tracks, instinct taking over. "What are we doing, Kip?" I hissed.

My sudden halt made Kip release my arm, but he still stood very close to me, breathing more heavily than a walk down a flight of stairs should have warranted. Especially for a man in his physical condition…and why was my mind going *there*, of all places?

Because I was confused and frightened, I told myself. Distraction: a powerful tool.

"Just come on," he said, reaching for my arm once more.

My chameleon sense was threatening to flare up and erase me. I danced back a step, keeping just away from him. "No. Kip, you have to tell me what's going on." I struggled to keep my voice somewhat normal. "Why are you trying to take me to that boat?"

"I told you we need to talk."

"So let's talk. Right here." I stood firm, glaring at him, though I could barely see him.

He released a heavy sigh. "Here, give me that," he said, reaching for my flashlight. I handed it to him with the unthinking obedience that the law-abiding give to the authorities. He flicked it off and tucked it away somewhere. "What are you doing sneaking over to Ms. Cannon's house after midnight?"

"I…" I stammered, my face flushing. "I needed to talk to her, and, um, it's been kind of hard to get hold of her by phone. I wanted to make sure she was all right."

Echoing my earlier thoughts, Kip said, "And if she weren't all right? What exactly were you going to do about it?"

"I would have called you, of course. Except—I tried that earlier, three times, and you didn't call me back. I'm confused, Kip. I don't know what to think. I'm just looking for answers."

He gave another frustrated sigh and took a few steps away from me on the rocky beach. My eyes began to adjust, letting me see a little bit more all the time. Kip's broad shoulders were hunched; he walked as if something pained him. Suddenly he wheeled around to face me again. "Cam, you are far from the only one in that situation." But then he straightened up, visibly getting hold of himself, clamping down on whatever bit of vulnerability he had just let slip. He stepped closer to me again, not touching me this time. "I just really need to know what you're doing out so late, and why you had to come over here."

"I told you," I said, still unsettled. "I was checking on Lisa. But if you say she's okay, I'll just go home now."

"No." The force in his voice halted me before I could even start walking away. "I think you know more than you're telling, about a lot of things."

A high, nervous laugh escaped me. You know, just because my body loves to find ever newer and more interesting ways to betray me. "I've told you everything I know about—all this," I said, waving my hands around vaguely in a pathetic attempt to distract us all from this blatant lie.

His eyes narrowed as he leaned even closer. He looked almost ominous in the weird starlight coming off the water. "Do you make it a practice to check on your neighbors regularly?"

"What?"

"Or did you have some specific reason for thinking she might *not* be all right?"

"I…" I couldn't tell him about her weird phone call. Or could I? "She just, I don't know—this has all been really scary for her, and…"

"Why did you need to see her so desperately?" he pressed. I could feel the heat of his breath on my face. "In the *middle of the night*?"

He was close enough to kiss me, still talking in a harsh whisper even though we were far from anyone who might possibly overhear. I felt a terrible pull towards him, something deep and undeniable. And he was scaring the hell out of me.

"I just…" I tried to take a step back, but he took hold of both my upper arms again. A twinge of pain went through my wound, and I sucked in a breath. "Kip, you're hurting me—and scaring me." *And I want you to kiss me, and I don't know what to do with that.*

He let go of my arms but stayed close, intense. "*Why did you need to see Lisa?"*

"I don't have to tell you *anything*." I clamped my mouth shut.

"As a matter of fact, you do. I am an officer of the law. You can answer me here, privately, or I can take you in and book you and you can answer me then, with a bunch of other people around and everything going into the public record."

"Book me for *what*?" My heart pounded. I stared back at him, rabbit in the headlights. "She...asked me for a favor. Something she wanted me to keep secret."

"So you admit you're holding secrets."

I shook my head, wildly. "Nothing that has anything to do with any of this. Something personal. Kip, she trusted me, don't make me betray that trust."

"You're lying."

I kept staring back at him, trying not to panic. Because of course, even though I was finally telling the truth, I also *was* lying. Lisa's secrets had everything to do with this. Her secrets had been stolen and hidden on that boat. Her secrets that were now safe under my mattress.

She trusted me. And I had to talk to her, before I could tell Kip or anyone else anything. "Kip, just let me go home."

"No, Cam, I can't do that. If you can't tell me what this *favor* is for Lisa, then I need to keep you with me."

"What?" I gaped at him. "Why?"

"Because I need answers. Until you can tell me everything you know, and I mean *everything*, you're with me."

"Where *is* Lisa?" I blurted out, without even really meaning to. "Is she really home, is she really all right? Why were you lurking in the dark on her porch?"

Kip let out an angry huff of breath. "She's fine. She gave us several statements, and then told us she was going to take a sedative and try to get some sleep, that she has been sleeping poorly lately, because of all the intrigue. She asked if I could leave a deputy at her house to ensure that she wasn't disturbed during the night. I

decided to do it myself. I was curious to see who might show up."
He stalked away from me again a few steps on the cold beach.
"Does that satisfy you, Ms. Tate? Are you ready to stop interro-
gating *me* now?"

"Kip, don't be this way," I said. "We're friends, and I care about
Lisa. Aren't we all on the same team here?"

He shook his head, in frustration rather than disagreement, it
seemed. "I would like to think so," he said. Then he looked up
at me, his expression unreadable. Closed. "Unfortunately, I don't
have the luxury of making such assumptions."

"What? What do you mean?"

He looked at me intently. "Come along. Maybe the boat will
jog your memory." He reached out for my arm once more.

"Really, truly," I protested, "I promise I'll go straight back to
bed and not leave till—"

"No." He hauled me forward, not violently but not gently
either. "You're coming with me. Everything peculiar that's happened around here started when you arrived on the island. Everything was under control until your arrival, and you seem like
such a nice person, Ms. Tate. But I can no longer ignore all these
unlikely coincidences and 'accidents'."

"*What?*" I stopped dead in my tracks again, no matter that he
was still trying to yank on my arm. "What are you talking about,
Kip Rankin?"

He stopped too, turning to face me on the dark shore. "Island
life was peaceful and quiet before you got here. It was almost
boring." He snorted. "I'd take boring again, in a heartbeat. Now
I've got…" He trailed off, waving an arm helplessly. "You appear
at the heart of everything unsettling going on around here. On
my island. You bat your innocent eyes at me, at everyone, and all
the while more people are dropping dead. What am I supposed
to make of that?"

"I don't know!" I cried. "It's nothing to do with me! You have
to believe me!"

"I don't *have* to believe anything. And I would like to know who you're working for."

"I work for the *Brixtons*!" My voice was almost a wail.

"I find that highly unlikely." He tightened his grip and started us down the shore again; I stumbled along beside him, so he'd stop pulling so hard on my sore arm.

He led me to the police line tape, reaching out and yanking it down without pausing. I struggled to keep up, trying not to trip on the tape in the dark. "Come on," he said again, leading me onto the dock and the side of the boat.

"Kip—" I started to say, and the boat rocked.

"Get on." He shoved me at the edge of the boat; I grabbed at it in a panic. I would have fallen into the water otherwise. "Get *on*!" he growled.

"But there's—this is a crime scene."

"That's never stopped you before, has it?" He gave me another push, so I scrambled over the side and onto the cluttered deck of the boat, almost tripping over a very familiar grocery bag...and some half-empty ziplocks. *The leftovers!* But who...?

I turned and faced him. Kip leapt on after me, grabbing my arm again and trying to drag me toward the cabin.

"Wait—"

But he didn't listen, just flung open the cabin door and, holding me close to his side, pointed my flashlight at the still-open trapdoor in the floor. "I know it was you nosing down here, after we'd searched and found nothing. What was in there?"

"Kip—"

"*What did you find?*"

"Kip! There's someone on this boat!"

I heard a snort, but it was not Kip.

Someone stood at the back of the cabin, holding a big, shiny gun pointed right at us. "Yeah," she said with a smirk. "She's right. There's somebody on here, Deputy Dim Bulb."

It was Sheila.

CHAPTER 13

I'd never chameleoned from inside someone's grasp before, but I did it now. And since one of the effects of chameleoning—my earliest, youngest method of self-defense—was to make everyone in a very dangerous room forget about me, that's what happened.

It could have been funny, if it wasn't so terrifying.

Kip relaxed his grip on me, somehow forgetting I was even there. Sheila trained her gun on him. I, however, was one frozen chameleon, and could not slither away from him even if I'd thought that would be a good idea.

Sheila was there, alive and breathing, a crazy not-actually-dead-after-all lady with a gun.

"You..." Kip stammered, sounding deeply confused.

Sheila still smirked, but she too looked uncertain. It's not perfect, this supernatural disability of mine. Everyone affected by it knows they're missing something...they just can't quite put their fingers on what.

When I'd done this before with Sheila, it had pissed her off. It worked just the same this time. Sadly for Kip, he was the only one she knew to focus on.

"Yeah, me," she snarled at him, waggling the gun a little. "Thought I was out of your hair, did you?"

"You can't...be here," he stammered.

She tried again for her smirk. "Seems like I can." I could see her finger tighten on the trigger. Was she going to *shoot* him? A cop? Just how stupid *was* she?

Still pressed against Kip as I was, I could feel him reach for his gun. He thought I was dangerous, but he'd been holding me against his holstered gun. He couldn't have thought I was *that* dangerous. He actually had to push against me to get enough leverage to reach it.

I struggled to regain my visibility, my voice. I had to return to presence in this room. This terrifying, tiny room. With two armed, unstable people in it. Well, one unstable person; and one who was confusing the hell out of me at the moment.

I had never had any control of my "gift"…until last week. Then, I was able to intentionally bring on the chameleoning, in order to save my life.

Could I do the same thing in reverse, now? For the same reason? Could I…bring myself back to visibility?

I could only try. I breathed deeply. I focused on my core and pulled calm back into my body. Into my limbs. Into my mind.

Meanwhile, Kip had his gun out, aimed at Sheila. His arm was steady against my side, but when he spoke, his voice shook. "You're under arrest. Drop it, Sheila."

She merely raised her own gun higher, now aiming directly between his eyes. "You wouldn't dare," she hissed. "Stupid country cop, have you ever shot anyone in your whole damn life? Stuck out here on this backwater island writing tickets for tourists and giving directions. You couldn't shoot a squirrel, Deputy Doofus."

She was *goading* him. Did she *want* to die?

I drew calm into myself. Again, again. I watched everything, and pulled calm from the universe, into me.

My left elbow, the one touching Kip, started to tingle.

Sheila kept going. Her voice sounded ragged. "Go on and do it. Stop being Howdy Doody in a uniform, and start being a cop. Do it."

"Don't tempt me, you traitorous, lying gargoyle."

I'd never heard such anger and ugliness in Kip's voice. Kip's golden, mellifluous voice. Was the man I'd known, the man I'd grown to like and trust, just a fiction? Was this the real Kip?

My whole left side came alive, tingling and sparking as the nerves fired. I tried to clear my throat, coming up with a faint squeak.

Kip and Sheila both turned to me. Because I had popped right back into existence for them. They were both shocked and confused. Surprise was on my side. "This has to *stop*," I said, as forcefully as I could. My voice still faltered, but they could hear it, and I could use it, I was *visible*, I'd done it! "Put your guns away. Now."

Sheila just stared at me, open-mouthed. Even though she'd seen my chameleon trick before, she looked like she'd been pole-axed. Kip, however...his gun arm, still tightly pressed against my side, faltered a little. Was he beginning to lower it? Was this actually going to work?

The boat jolted as someone jumped on board, out on the deck behind us. "Hands up, all of you!"

Kip's hand shot upward again and I felt him fire, I felt the strong report of the gun reverberate through his arm and my side. The impact of it broke whatever was left of my frozenness; I dropped to the floor, trying yet again to make myself as small as possible, only deliberately this time. Gunshots sang out all around me—I couldn't tell if it was Sheila firing, Kip again, or the new player, whoever that was. Or all of them at once. I cringed further and made for the corner.

"I SAID HANDS UP," bellowed Deputy Sherman, slamming the tiny cabin door open. "DROP YOUR WEAPONS, BOTH OF YOU!"

The boat rocked again. More people were boarding.

"No!" screamed Sheila, turning the gun on herself.

I was on my feet and hurling myself at her before I could even think. I cannonballed into her, knocking the gun away from her face. She managed to squeeze the trigger before it clattered away from her, but she didn't hit herself. Or me.

I fervently hoped the bullet hadn't caught anyone. There'd been quite enough stray-bullet wounds around here lately, thank you very much.

Sheila hauled back and slugged me in the chin; entangled as we were on the floor, she wasn't able to get much force behind the blow, but I saw stars all the same. "You dumb hairdresser bitch!" she hissed in my ear. She groaned in anger or pain. Maybe she had caught herself with the bullet. "I'm the dummy. Here I was, trying to protect you."

"Sheila," I groaned. "Please, please stop trying to protect me. Really."

"You two! Move apart and raise your hands!" Deputy Sherman hollered. I looked up to see that she'd somehow disarmed and subdued Kip...and she hadn't done it alone.

Behind Sherman stood a tall, thin woman in head-to-toe black except for the bold white "FBI" emblazoned across her chest, made even taller by a sizable natural do shaved high and tight above her ears. She looked like Grace Jones in an FBI jacket. She towered over a smaller man in the unmistakable scarlet uniform of the Royal Canadian Mounted Police.

"Deputy Rankin, you are relieved of your duties in this investigation until further notice," the FBI agent intoned. "Inspector McMichaels and I are in charge from now on."

Kip groaned, leaning against the cabin wall. "I was only trying to get to the bottom of things..." He shook a finger at me. "She's...she's in this somehow."

The FBI agent turned to Sherman. "Bring them in. Cuff him if you need to." She pointed at Sheila. "Definitely cuff her. And bring the civilians too."

Sherman complied, perhaps even a little eagerly. Kip didn't fight her. As the agent and the Mountie hauled him to his feet, he gave me a long last look, a look that conveyed regret, panic, desperation. He laid a finger against his lips in a clear signal, then let them handcuff him without a trace of struggle. He didn't want me to tell them *anything*.

I'd never been so confused in my life.

They frog-marched him out of the tiny cabin as Sherman closed in on Sheila, who looked cornered, panicked, like she was ready to make a break for it. Sherman kept her gun trained and steady. "Don't even think about it. Even if you run, we won't shoot you. Not to kill, anyway. You're going to talk to us this time." Sheila's face hardened. Kip was right. She did look like a gargoyle. But it was shocking that he'd ever say something so cruel.

"You, whoever you really are. Come on," Sherman said to me with a scoff. "Party at the Orcas Island Substation." And then she gave me a smirk that rivaled any Sheila had ever come up with.

Who *was* this Deputy Sherman, anyway?

And wait—she had said *civilians*? Who were the civilians, besides me?

"Testy, testy," came JoJo's voice from the boat's deck. "No need to haul on me like that. *I* called *you*, didn't I?"

"Come along, Mr. Brixton," I heard the Mountie say. "We'll sort this all out downtown."

"Downtown" my foot, I thought. In a county without a single stoplight.

☙

It was hours later and the sky was getting light when I rode home in the backseat of Deputy Sherman's car. JoJo sat to my right, trying to keep up his usual light and flirtatious banter. "So what drew you to law enforcement, Deputy Sherman? The handcuffs?"

Deputy Sherman was having none of it.

I wondered where Kip and Sheila were. With the FBI agent and/or the Mountie? After what I'd been through, my concern for the two of them confused me. I'd been manhandled by the courtliest man I'd ever met, and "protected" almost to death by a woman who had murdered a man right before my eyes and trained a gun on me more than once. Still, I couldn't stop wondering where they were. Were they being held longer than us, or booked, or transported to—somewhere else?

I'd repeated my side of the story so many times, I could hear it in my brain on a loop. I was worried about Lisa Cannon. So I walked over to check on her. Kip Rankin intercepted me, and insisted I go with him to the boat. I had no idea why. There, we encountered Sheila and after that, things were a confusing blur. No, I had no idea why Kip wanted me on that boat. Yes, I'd been on the boat before, looking for my cat, and I was so sorry I hadn't told anyone about it. Yes, I'd pulled up the floorboards, because James was somehow trapped in there. No, I hadn't seen or found anything under that floor, besides my cat.

I wasn't telling anyone that part.

I was in trouble for disturbing a possible crime scene. I was a person of interest. I was not to leave the island. But I'd stayed calm, that was the important thing. No chameleoning at all, no strange erasures that would alarm everyone in the police station. I was sure a police station, even one on a tiny island at the edge of everything, had cameras everywhere. What would happen if my supernatural disability were captured on tape? *Could* it be captured on tape?

"You know, I left the island because it was boring," JoJo murmured. "This has been the least boring family holiday in memory." He sounded bemused.

I looked over at his profile, handsome and golden in the dawn. I wondered what it would be like to have so much of what he had—money, looks, that gorgeous build—and not know what to do with yourself. He didn't seem to do much besides drink and flirt. It seemed like a colossal waste.

Exhaustion had made me judgey. At least he was helpful.

"Thank you."

"She speaks." He smiled at me. "But what are you thanking me for?"

"For calling for help. I have no idea how you knew something was wrong, but however you knew it, you got me out of a bad situation. So thank you."

He gave a rueful smile and shook his head. "I can't claim any psychic superpowers. It appears we were both worried about Lisa. I was headed over to check on her myself. I saw Rankin man-handling you in a way that was not professional. And no matter what you might say about Kip Rankin, he's always the soul of professionalism. Something was definitely wrong. So I put in a call on a back channel."

I didn't even know what a back channel was, but I was glad such a thing existed.

I thought about my family holiday weekend and stared out the window, watching for the waters of Massacre Bay. I would see morning light dancing on the water through the trees, soon.

We pulled up to the Brixton gate, which was closed. "Pull up to the keypad," JoJo said, as offhand as if he were addressing a cab driver. "Could you roll down this window? Never mind. I'll get out." He tried the handle. "Could you let me *out*? *Now*?" He panicked. Of all the happenings of the weekend, finding a dead body, burglary, finding another dead body, Kip's going rogue, Sheila being alive, and the arrival of the RCMPs and the FBI, the thing that got him the most upset was being trapped in the back of a police vehicle.

I felt exactly the same way.

When Deputy Sherman released us from the car, neither of us wanted to get back in. He waved her off, and we walked silently toward the houses. I could see the waters of Massacre Bay, and they were as just beautiful as I'd imagined.

I found myself leaning against JoJo as we walked. "JoJo? I can't understand why you'd ever want to leave. I love it here."

He put his arm around my shoulder in a companionable way.

"Then you can have it. I'll be on the next ferry out."

I smiled for the first time in at least a day. He let go of me and went toward the big house, and I walked on to mine. I could hear Diana Brixton's voice as he opened the door, and had no desire whatsoever to know what she was saying.

Maybe I *could* understand JoJo's desire to leave here, after all.

ᏊᎧ

The Intruder was still dominating the driveway, of course, as silent and huge and out of place as ever. My car and my parents' Lexus were next to (oddly enough) Jen's white van. Maybe she'd come over to keep my parents company while I was at the station. The kitchen light shone through the guesthouse window. I hoped they hadn't been up all night. I'd asked Deputy Sherman to give them a call, but had no idea whether or not she actually had. She'd spent most of the night looking slightly smug, as if she'd always known something was strange about Kip Rankin, and now we *all* knew.

"Brrup?" A familiar little heart-shaped face popped up on the path before me. James, with a dead shrew dangling from his mouth.

I shuddered. "Don't I feed you enough?" At least it wasn't a bird. He darted towards the door as I tried to open it. "No, James, you're not bringing that inside. James!" He turned and sped away, unwilling to surrender his prize catch.

When I stepped into the kitchen, my parents were seated at the table with coffee, both their faces pale and concerned. My mother burst immediately into tears.

"Oh Mom, I'm fine." But they were on me, enfolding me in their arms. "Dad, please. I'm *fine*." But it felt so good that I was crying, too.

My dad's arms were shaking, and so was his voice. "I don't buy that for a minute. Cliff had to leave on the ferry to make his flight, but he agrees with us. We're taking you home with us."

"Dad…"

"No arguing! Your mom and I have gotten you a ferry reservation. You're coming back to Wenatchee with us. It's settled."

I let myself live there for about thirty seconds. Because it felt so *easy*, the idea of getting into my car, driving to the ferry, leaving these weeks of Orcas intrigue behind. It would be so easy, wouldn't it? I wouldn't have to put up with Diana Brixton and her salt suspicions and her instruction manual. I wouldn't have to worry about finishing the play, and live through the prospect of watching it bomb onstage because the actors were so out of control or it just plain sucked. I wouldn't have to untangle whatever mystery was behind Lisa and that binder, and her ex-husband, and her homicidal ex-employee. I wouldn't have to deal with my confusing feelings for Kip, especially in light of the last night. And whatever the deeper mysteries of Orcas were, these boats and bodies, these mysteries could carry on without me. It was just too much.

Except…

I pulled myself out of my tangle of parental love and tears and hugs. "I can't leave. And I don't want to."

"But Cam…" My mom shook her head. "You're not *safe* here."

"I've spent too much of my life trying to be safe, Mom. I've only learned how to hide. I mean, no one is as good at hiding as I am. You know that, right?"

My mother blinked. My father squeezed my shoulder, then handed me a cup of coffee.

"I have to learn another way. I have to figure out how to stop hiding all the time. And I think this is the right place to do it. Here, on Orcas Island." I searched my parents' eyes, expecting to find disappointment. Instead I saw a flicker of understanding, a small nod, the slightest hint of a smile.

In spite of themselves, my parents were proud.

Dad started to zip up his bulky sweater. "Well, if you're staying, then I'd better unpack your car, Cam."

"You packed my *car*?"

My mother patted me. "Your father couldn't sleep. It gave him something to do."

I looked out the window. Jen's truck was still there by mine. "Do you guys know where Jen is? Why is her van here?"

The room went very quiet, and my parents exchanged looks. "Er. I'm...going to go get your bags."

What the heck?

I watched my father head out to my car, which was unlocked, apparently. He was swinging out my bag when the door to the Intruder opened. I watched as Jen looked out, testing the morning air. Jen, with hair tousled, cheeks flushed, smiling barefoot and wearing a very familiar T-shirt, one that belonged to...

Kevin.

Kevin, who stood close behind her, Kevin who wrapped an arm around her waist while handing her a cup of coffee, no doubt brewed in his magical Magnavox coffee system, Kevin who was wearing only his boxer briefs, Kevin who smiled sweetly into Jen's face as she came in for a kiss, the only kind of kiss Kevin gave in the morning before he'd brushed his teeth. A sweet little closed-lips morning kiss with those sweet, full, perfect lips of his.

"Oh." The word slipped out of me, along with a tiny weight I hadn't even known I was still carrying. "*Oh.*" I felt nearly giddy with sudden clarity, and vertigo. I raised my coffee cup to my best friend in a silent toast, but I couldn't smile.

Jen turned to look at the house, her expression suddenly worried, and caught my eye through the window. She gave me a tremulous smile, a question of a smile.

I made myself smile at her, as my heart spun in—confusion, pain...relief? All of it.

Her eyes widened. Then she raised her own cup back to me.

<<<>>>

Recipes

CRANBERRY JELLO SALAD
2 small packages raspberry gelatin mix
2 cups boiling water
Dissolve gelatin mix in water but do NOT add any cold water
Stir in:
1 can whole cranberry sauce
1 large can crushed pineapple—juice and all
1 cup chopped pecans
After the gelatin sets up, spread the top with a mixture of cream cheese and sour cream, blended together till creamy. Serve atop leaves of iceberg lettuce, on the good china.

MASHED POTATOES
The secret is mayonnaise.

TOP OF THE STOVE STUFFING
Prep time: 25 minutes
Ingredients:
2.5 cups of bread cubes; either homemade from artisan bread (if you're Kevin) or with store-bought bread cubes (if you're anyone else).
3 tbs unsalted butter
1 rib of celery, chopped
1 small onion, finely chopped
2 cloves garlic, minced
2 tbs fresh parsley (if you're Kevin) or 1 tbs dried parsley (if you're anyone else).
½ tsp sage
¼ tsp marjoram
⅛ tsp pepper
¼ tsp kosher salt (You can sub regular salt if you're not Kevin).

1¼ cups chicken stock; either homemade (if you're Kevin) or canned (if you're anyone else).

Making the Stuffing
Dice the celery and onion into a single bowl.
In a large sauce pan, melt the butter and kosher salt over medium heat. Add the celery, onion and garlic. Cook until the veggies are softened and the onion starts to become translucent. Roughly 5 minutes. Add the herbs, spices and chicken stock to the mix and stir. Bring to a boil. Once the mixture hits a rolling boil, add the bread cubes. Quickly mix in the cubes to the liquid, cover and remove from heat. Let sit covered for 5 minutes. Fluff the mixture with a fork before serving.
Variations: Add one cup of sauteed fresh sliced or chopped mushrooms at Step 4.

PEAR AND PERSIMMON CHUTNEY
(courtesy of Kevin's English friend Chaz)

3 lb. firm Fuyu persimmons, peeled, seeded and finely chopped
2 lb. pears, peeled and finely chopped
1 onion, finely chopped
2" piece ginger, peeled and grated
1/2 cup raisins
2/3 cup molasses sugar
1/3 cup honey
1/2 cup apple cider vinegar
juice of a lemon
1 heaped tbsp. mustard seeds
1 heaped tbsp. coriander seeds
heaped 1/2 tsp. garam masala
heaped 1/2 tsp. curry powder
1 heaped tsp. red pepper flakes
salt to taste

Put everything into the same pot, bring to the boil and simmer for an hour or so, until sticky and thick. Pour into hot sterilised jars and seal according to the customs of your country. Enjoy with cold meats and hard cheeses.

Sneak Preview of

ORCAS INVESTIGATION
Book 3 of the Chameleon Chronicles

CHAPTER 1

Felicia: It's such a dark and stormy night.

It wasn't dark, though, or stormy, or night. I deleted the line and sighed, staring out my kitchen window. I'd moved my laptop in here because the room was brighter and cheerier than the little bedroom I'd designated as an office, but the writing wasn't going any better in here.

I got up and poured another cup of coffee and brought it back to the table, so I could stare out the window a little longer. Outside was an icescape, brilliantly beautiful, lethal. Which didn't stop a small cottontail rabbit from hopping across the moss "lawn," pausing to nibble here and there. Something startled him; he darted away, showing me a flash of white tail as he went.

Felicia: I don't know how to untangle this mystery. I want to go to bed and pull the covers over my head.

Delete, delete.

I sipped my coffee and watched the rabbit cautiously edge his way back over the frozen moss. Didn't he freeze his little paws? Probably everything he was finding to eat was crunchy. It had been below freezing here for nearly a week, starting right after the...eventful...Thanksgiving weekend. Right after everyone left. Leaving me here, alone in a three-bedroom guesthouse be-hind an I-can't-count-that-high-bedroom mansion owned by my employers, the Brixtons.

Well, at least it wasn't raining. But it had been so very, *very* cold. I was entirely out of my meager supply of firewood, and praying for the power to stay on so that at least my central heat-ing would remain operational. After a hair-raising trip to town the first day, I hadn't dared to drive on the ice again.

I wasn't going to starve, though. The Thanksgiving leftovers would keep me going for another week, easy. Even without all the extra food that my parents and Kevin had brought.

Kevin...

Felicia: I think about my ex-boyfriend only very occasionally, and only when I'm unfortunately reminded of his existence. I simply do not have time for such nonsense, because I

Ugh. Delete, delete, delete.

I took another sip of coffee and stared at my silent cell phone beside the computer. Sooner or later, I was going to have to call my friend Jen. My former new best friend who had taken off with my ex-boyfriend, Kevin, in his Intruder...nope, not going there. Not yet. Kevin and I were done. He and Jen...it hurt, but I was okay. I wished them well.

I really did.

But it made it awfully quiet around here.

But quiet was good! I had a play to finish writing, and by "fin-ish" I meant "write the second and third acts and revise the first act." The long (cold!) dark nights and short (cold!) days of winter should be giving me plenty of time to work on it.

Instead, I was writing—and deleting—stupid lines and point-less stage directions and basically diary entries, knowing even as I wrote them that they were not part of this story, but the words bubbled out all the same. The wrong words. So many wrong words.

I got up and paced around the house, checking the thermostat as I went through the living room, inching it up another degree. Gazing sadly into the empty, dark fireplace. Jen was going to help me find seasoned firewood—*seasoned*, that meant old and dry and long-dead, not fresh-cut, not rain-soaked. Not frozen solid. See how much I was learning about rural life already?

James glanced up from where he'd been sleeping on the couch, gave me a half-heartedly inquisitive *meow*, and returned to slumber. He'd been much more of a homebody since everyone had left. Or maybe it was just the cold snap. I think he did like the quiet and solitude, though; or maybe he was just growing up. Though he had a ways to go. He was barely the equivalent of a teenager, in cat years. All legs and mischief and appetite.

I paced back into the kitchen. My blank screen, *ACT TWO* in bold and Italics at the top of it, stared back at me.

Felicia: I must get out of this house, or I'll go stark raving mad.

Delete. Delete. Delete.

"Okay, Cam," I said to myself, as I stood in front of the open fridge that I had no memory of opening, much less walking over to. "I don't know about Felicia, but you are not cut out for the cabin-fever lifestyle." I had to go to town, to see another human being, to do *something*. After all the drama and intrigue and madness since I'd arrived here on Orcas Island, to have had everything suddenly go so quiet and peaceful…it was intolerable.

But I couldn't drive on that ice. My little Honda just couldn't handle it, even with the chains I didn't really know how to put on.

And I had nobody to call for help.

I hadn't realized how much I'd relied on my little community of friends and neighbors, until they'd all vanished. My family, of course, had only been visiting for the weekend, as had the Brixtons (and their…interesting…children, JoJo and Clary). But my island friends…Colin, who'd taken a contract job in San Diego for the winter, taking his boat and sailing away. Lisa Cannon, also off-island, tending to mysterious business in Seattle. Jen…

yeah, Jen.

And Kip. I supposed Kip was a friend, no matter that he'd confused me so terribly right when it all went down on Snooks's boat. Kip, San Juan County Deputy Sheriff, who I had last seen being hauled off in handcuffs by a very impressive FBI agent—and, if that weren't enough, a Canadian Mountie as well.

I still couldn't quite get my head around the fact that Kip was a crooked cop. He was the most straight-laced guy I knew, with rugged good looks and that mellifluous voice. But I couldn't deny the evidence of my own senses. Kip had waylaid me and tried to drag me off to the strange, abandoned boat, all the while accusing me—vaguely—of being somehow behind all the intrigue Orcas had been experiencing of late. Of harboring secrets.

Well, that last part was true, a bit. But they weren't my secrets, and they really shouldn't have been the cause of any of our handful of dead bodies.

Felicia paces the stage, out of her mind with boredom.

Felicia: Maybe if I just drive really slowly and carefully, I can make it to town and back without sliding off the road and into the sound. It's movie night at the Seaview, after all; and I'm nearly out of cream.

Delete, delete, but I wasn't wrong, was I? The sun was already setting, I'd gotten no writing done today, the icepocalypse was never going to melt, and semi-first-run movies played only two nights a week here. I'd missed last night, being too scared to drive. If I didn't go tonight, I'd not get to see the new Marvel release at all.

Unless I went to the mainland—"America". Not likely.

So that's how I found myself bundling up against the cold, preparing to crunch across the frozen driveway to my iced-shut car. I wound a plaid muffler (a Pendleton, a real thrift shop score) over my head and around my neck, and put on my wool peacoat. That would do it, yes? I'd be protected by all this wool if I slid off the road and landed in the ditch and it was too icy to walk out for help and no one passed my car for hours because every other resident of this icy, remote island was too sensible to leave home on a night like this?

What was I thinking?

I was thinking that I was going stir-crazy. And needed diversion and human interaction. Like, you know, a normal person would. And that a movie would be good for me. It would take me out of my own head, which was preoccupied with personal disappointment and the strange goings-on that I had no real explanation for. Like Sheila, and how she'd come back from the dead. And Lisa's binder, and how strange it was that she'd been desperate for me to find it, but completely unconcerned about getting it back from me.

And those strange gifts at my back door, where I heard a knock. A knock?

Company, in this weather?

I headed back through the house to the kitchen, where I opened the door to the most peculiar old woman I'd ever seen. She was tall, though she'd clearly been even more statuesque when she was younger (like, less than eighty-five); and she was swathed head to toe in turbulent, dramatic colors. I think it was a coat, once; now it was an assortment of fire-engine red boiled wool underneath; patches of purple and green on the sleeves; a black-and-white polka dot belt, eight inches wide at least; and what could only be epaulettes on both shoulders. Epaulettes that didn't match, even sort of: a tight military braid on one side; a tasseled, hand-sewn number on the other. She had hair white as snow (but had she cut it herself? Oh please no), milky blue eyes, and a strong mouth adorned with lipstick to match the first layer of her coat.

This vision held out a gallon-sized jar of clearly homemade pickles, in a hand that did not tremble. *She must be way stronger than she looks*, I thought. "Hello, dear," she said, in a clear, forceful voice. "I thought it was about time I introduced myself. My name is Paige Berry, and I find myself in a bit of a pickle." My eyes dropped to the jar of pickles in her hand; she raised a white eyebrow and lifted her lips in the ghost of a smile. "Yes, I know, a pun of an introduction, isn't it? But I'm talking about a real pickle. I find myself in a serious *situation*, Ms. Tate."

Another *situation*? My heart sank. "How serious?"

"Very serious." Her pale blue eyes fixed mine with an oddly commanding stare. "I'm hoping you can help me with it. I understand you have a way with mysteries."

"They seem to find me," I blurted. "Well—come in," I added. We were both heavily bundled up, but I could still feel the iciness colonizing my house.

"Thank you." She thrust the pickle jar at me; I took it, needing both hands for the weight. "From my garden," she said, as I wrestled the jar to the counter and set it down. No wonder she'd needed such a huge jar; these had been made from the biggest cucumbers in creation. "I'm out of the fresh stuff, but I had time to put up a few dozen jars before the deep freeze." As I closed the kitchen door, she glanced around appraisingly, her eyes lighting on the coffee pot. "Well, well. Pour me a cup, and get comfortable. This may take a while."

Acknowledgments

The imaginary Laura Gayle thanks the very real authors, Shannon Page and Karen G. Berry, for letting her romp through a second Orcas book—with more to come. No one writes in a vacuum. Love and encouragement are only part of the support given by Mark and Tony, who tolerate the near-constant presence of laptops, notebooks, and abandoned cups of coffee brewed too early on weekend mornings.

Shannon and Karen wish to say thanks, again, to all the folks who helped with book one for their help on this sequel: proofing, editing, recipes, modeling, and more. For book two, they want to add thanks for the publication *Orcas Issues: News and Views*, most specifically for the weekly "Sheriff's Report" compilation. Not that anything in these books comes from real life. Of course not.

Photograph by Mark J. Ferrari

Laura Gayle is the nom de plume of two friends who were ready to collaborate.

Shannon Page was born on Halloween night and raised without television on a back-to-the-land commune in northern California. Her work has appeared in Clarkesworld, Interzone, Fantasy, Black Static, Tor.com, and many anthologies. Books include Eel River; Orcas Intrigue, the first book of the Chameleon Chronicles, co-written with Karen G. Berry; Our Lady of the Islands, co-written with the late Jay Lake; and the forthcoming The Queen and The Tower, book one of the Nightcraft Quartet. Her many editing credits include the essay collection The Usual Path to Publication and the anthology Witches, Stitches & Bitches. Shannon is a longtime yoga practitioner, has no tattoos, and recently moved with her husband, Mark Ferrari, to a house on Orcas Island, Washington, where she makes shrubs (aka sipping vinegars) when she's not making words. Visit her at www.shannonpage.net.

Karen G. Berry has lived in or near Portland, Oregon, for over thirty years. So far, she has failed to transcend her solidly Midwestern upbringing. She has three grown daughters, two small dogs, one fantastic partner named Tony, and several thousand books. A social media professional by day, Karen is an extensively published poet with work appearing in many print and online journals. Karen's first novel is Love and Mayhem at the Francie June Memorial Trailer Park. Her second novel is The Iris Files: Notes from a Desperate Housewife. Visit her at www.karengberry.mywriting.network/.

Made in the USA
Columbia, SC
26 June 2021